MISTAH KURTZ!

MISTAH KURTZ!

JAMES REICH

GRAND RAPIDS, MICHIGAN

Mistah Kurtz!
Copyright © 2016 by James Reich
ISBN: 978-0-9905733-6-4
Library of Congress Control Number: 2015953130

First Anti-Oedipal Paperback Edition, March 2016

www.RawDogScreaming.com

Cover Design © 2016 by James Reich
www.JamesReichBooks.com

Layout by D. Harlan Wilson
www.DHarlanWilson.com

Anti-Oedipus Press
Grand Rapids, MI

www.Anti-OedipusPress.com

ALSO BY JAMES REICH

Bombshell
I, Judas

For Henry Miller.

"Yes! It recedes. And this was the chance to afford one more view of it—even to my own eyes."

—Joseph Conrad

My Intended,

Nightfall, lavender to black—The cannibal in his rotting blue uniform has just cleared away the tea. Mosquitos rifled his skin. I watched them swarm over his ripped gold epaulettes as he gathered the remnants of the service. This evening, the moon is a mask in electroplate, wreathed in a nimbus of storm clouds as the figure of my boy hunches—*bereaved*. He is called Nsumbu. While he cleared up, I tracked a ribbon of malarial sweat spilling from the frayed cuffs of his field jacket, following the bones of his bull-black fingers. From these, I studied its drip, rolling down the stem of my spoon, descending into my teacup—mercury from a broken barometer. I witness my world as an outsider, slipping out of my skin, observing my pale alienage, my transit, and my station. Out there, the Company men are beetles pushing shit. They bore recklessly into the slop of the earth, hesitating only to witness the cryptic tunnel collapsing slowly behind them. I am a fly, buzzing my own embodiment, a thousand eye lenses aghast. What is Kurtz? Company man, poet, cannonball, or feral god—we shall find him out.

The last of my last Brussels porcelain is a delicate white vessel, rimmed with gold. It is decorated with a sepia painting of small boats sailing upon flat tidewater—strange to think it journeying with me from our home, as it might have been in London, now receiving the sweat of an African, falling as so many diamonds from the crushing cave of his soul. Outside in my rain garden, there is the skull of an infant that is not so translucent as this teacup when lifted to the light. Nsumbu is my singular friend and protégé. He wears no shirt beneath his blue coat. Manacle scars rise from his brown wrists, puckered as slugs on the dead. Sometimes, when I am dressing, his eyes trace over the pale remains of the strap scars my father gave me, these pearly stripes indicating the callous bars of imprisoned sympathy between us. Neither Nsumbu nor the dregs of his gang who lounge in the night are dangerous to me. My station is testament to a bloody equilibrium. My extremism in ivory collection announces it, and Nsumbu is witness to how far I will go. This latent violence mortifies our time and tenderness.

It had occurred to me to ask him to return the cup, so that I might lift it to my lips. In the undulating heat of this night, some perspiration from my skin would fall in after his—our common temper swirling in a vortex of sickness and wet leaves. His wicked salt would pass into me. We have already shared our shivering blood, a dynamite concussion charging me back through the fathoms of race to where we were both of us—once—the same insensate creature, mouthing piteously in the mutual mud of all our days. Inside a flare of lightning, Nsumbu had hesitated at the threshold of my hut, listening to the wind through the jungle. The tea service rattled as he inclined to me. "Good evening, Mistah Kurtz." Wordlessly, I watched him leave, brushing a crested gecko from the screen door. Thunder fulminates over the moonlit ferns. We have been here since the beginning of time. By now, it must be 1891. The veranda of my station house is decaying in the rain, gracile struts bending under the night. The windward side is shredding.

And these words may disintegrate with me, also. What an ivory tower this is, my kingdom of—

Ah, but here *She* comes, my black widow, weaving me into the deep and booming negritude of her soul. I will not give her away. It is cruel of me, so unspeakably cruel. Not now.

*The stilts of my wicker palace on the Lake—expert swimmers—*Nsumbu returns to my quarters as I am writing this, his absurd uniform soaked through from the deluge. The deep blue cloth strains against his frame, somehow muscular even in conditions of malnourishment. The rain here comes in sheets, green as the canvas shades at the windows. The boy's bare feet are slicked with mud, the scars on his ankles marking the tideline of clay. Moonlight furs him, tall, hesitant, breathing humid air in the open door. Neither of us can tell how old he is. He is another of the ageless things that swarm, and quite beautiful. I recall the day I picked him up in Kinshasa, his patient, cobra-like swaying, the gleam of the flames on his wide shoulders, and his dorsal muscles folding around like a hood. Beside my hammock, the kerosene lamp is almost out—a gentle hangover of paraffin drifts through my lungs. I watch him striking a match and lighting a candle stump. Through the fine gauze of my mosquito net, he stares at me, wondering if I am dead. There is always that chance, I suppose. I have heard that I am losing my mind in several languages: in adenoidal English, in the sultry glottal boom of the native tongue, and in clipped dry Russian. The jungle is a fine place to lose one's mind, but they are all wrong about me. Certainly, my ascension has been rapid. I have been stripping and scraping the waste away from my brain like a Roman legionnaire in his laconicum, shaving clay from his skin with a wet slate.

This afternoon, I had Nsumbu shave my head again, a pre-caution against infestation. I sat before the mirror, watching him brush the soap across my whitened hair—something else of me that you would not recognize—whetting the steel razor on a stone and washing it in a canteen of boiled water—memories of my father. My father had a face that belonged on the backside of coins, and a temper as simply tossed. Nsumbu has watched the slow darkening of my limbs with a quiet fascination. Tinged where I was pale, bleached where I was rich, I have become some kind of photographic negative. He watches for the creep of gangrene, or the lassi-tude of coma that have overwhelmed so many of what used to be my kind. The jungle is flecked with white corpses. I could not help but think of him drawing the razor across my throat as he shaved me, the blade biting the red meat of my neck—*Annihilating all that's made, To a green Thought in a green Shade*—I know that he is aware of our common origin, even if only by a near-fossilized instinct. I experienced this awareness in the manner in which he traced the contours of my scalp and skull with the blade, a primitive surgery, measuring me like one of the witch doctors of phrenology. Again, lightning snakes over the jungle and he is illumi-nated, still watching me from the doorway. As did Lazarus, I lift my fingers and part the veil of the mosquito net.

"Not yet, Nsumbu."

Something between a smile and a grimace blooms in peat-black face. He is doing his best to choke down an unspeakable grief. It is slow, his python-like assimilation of a monstrous prey.

"You brought our night-cap, boy?"

His white teeth revolve on a string of dried root as I hear the sharp clink of the bottles he has carried with him. For a moment the two effects fuse in me, as though his teeth are made of emerald glass.

"Good man." I swing my feet from the creaking thongs of my bed, and motion that he should remove his saturated coat by fingering imaginary buttons at my throat. As though observing some taboo surrounding the notion of his being bare-chested in my quarters, he shakes his head. The bottles are still held in the crook of his right arm, and the candle in his left hand. I foresee the white wax running onto his skin and Nsumbu letting the champagne fall in shock. Hastily, I reach forward and pull the bottles from him. Did he wince at my lunge, or the candle? The champagne bottles sound like chain links, the cork and overflow will sound like distant gunfire over Stanley Falls. This is a cosmos of fear in which I alone am not afraid. Uncertainty infects every blade of grass and every guilty tear. Yet, I remember it also on the green edge of dawn in the mist of Charleville where I was born, running with dew close to France's border with Belgium, lifting the reptilian roof tiles, shrugging like a whore under eaves, and rising as smoke from the squatting yellow dragon of the church. All creatures, all things outside myself swim in this dim, glistening and ever-present fear, spiraling outward with shivering arms like a galaxy seen through the empty streams of space.

This is the Congo.

I am the Government of the Abyss.

*Avenues of palms and sunken eyes—condensed milk—a stretcher—*My Intended, it has fallen to me to make the account. I recognize that I have become the cynosure of the Company, and that the bureaucratic anxieties of the King and Europe are fixed here. Far behind me, they are constructing a railway to run inland through the jungle beside the rapids, from Matadi and the Crystal Cliffs to Stanley Pool. Men will travel less fatally to the inner channels to stations such as this. Yet, even as I write, skeletons rattle beside the nascent track, reaching from the scorched grass. Dead masks gape as the building of it grinds on with dynamite and rust. Adhering thinly to the bone, their brown faces are collapsed and sunken. Birds have shucked the eyes. Wild animals have insulted the flesh, ripping out limbs and opening flyblown cavities in the torsos. Beside me, were you a fly on my wall, you would see the gold-embossed Company ledger that is my *Report on the Suppression of Savage Customs*. That, I have given up. There is nothing more to say. I can tell you that Nsumbu's sorrows are as real as that of any white man, as real as mine, and that we do what little we can for one another. I have gone beyond the point of accounting my ivory and the humdrum sins of the forest. On the other side of my desk are the rest of these papers that you must have in hand, the dark water that I cannot pretend will bring you comfort. I will tell you more of that journey, from Charleville to the Congo, in time. In London, I swore that I would tell you about how I lived before we met, always promising, yet finding ways to avoid delivering what is your due. The shame would throttle me. Perhaps, from this fond distance, I can speak, as I could not that afternoon in your father's study when he interrogated me and I daydreamed of strangulation and his popping eyes on the carpet. For the moment, as great membranous bats glide across this African night, and you might see me here, reposing in my hammock, know that somewhere beyond that railway and the mountains of quartz, beyond the imperturbable river, I am dead.

She is standing in the blue moonlight with Nsumbu. Inside an impenetrable sorrow, they are facing one another. That pallid glow illuminates her strong jaw when she turns to face my window, confident, certain that I am watching, as she reaches down, between Nsumbu's knotted thighs. His abject uniform lies in the long grass. She wears a necklace of sharp teeth.

Glittering soil on the sky tonight—it falls, ripping the station roof—I wonder what else will become of me, *le nègre blanc,* the White Negro—Will there be notice of my transit in the *Courriers des Ardennes?* What will you say bathed in the long shadow of my shame, with no grave and no body to lay in it? Perhaps it does not matter. Dead then. This work is my ghost. I nearly included the one photograph of myself, with the portrait of you. Perhaps it was because some fragment of my consciousness revolted at the idea of never being seen again. In the picture, I was thirteen, half my life away. I looked like a sullen child *roué*, refusing combs, and now there is an empty frame in the forest. I had thought of pinning it to a tree and watching it fade away, as with so many other vanishing totems here. Nailing myself to the mast appealed to me. Yet, either way, I cannot get it back.

There are two-dozen of us remaining at the station—many of the Negroes having fled during the fallow interregnum following my predecessor's death, when bizarre species arose, some curious about who would manage the ivory next, some resuscitating their rituals in the Company's place, and some merely too lethargic and downtrodden to run. As I write, the Russian interloper is outside, emitting his bizarre squeaks at the dark, seeking to seduce the moonlit bats. Nikolai Junker—he's a young mongrel, like me. I watched him, last evening, waiting under the parasol of a raffia palm, holding a candle, and deliberately surrounding his body in a typhoon of silver moths. I think that in his swarm, scorching their wings on his spark, Nikolai Junker was singing, either to himself or to the menacing wilderness beyond our kremlin of skulls and sticks. I could not say for certain. Years ago, he had been a physician, traipsing through the winter outskirts of Moscow, probably between frozen bodies, carrying his leather satchel of drugs and instruments. I picture him wrapped in an oversized bearskin coat, a thick fur Cossack's hat pulled down low on his brow, leaning into the wind, knocking on the rotting doors of pestilence. His blue eyes are set deep in sockets rimmed brown. The snowflakes melt, becoming thick African moths, wings humming. Thin blonde hair sweeps his tall forehead. The red bricks of his past are the twisted limbs of his future. His clothes, a chimeric uniform of rags, militaria, a torn flag, and sackcloth, flap on his willowy frame. Despite the colorful absurdity of his attire, it is difficult to resist succumbing to the idea that Junker still has some ice in his veins. The door of his reason is hanging by one buckled hinge. He has, of late, demanded more and more of my attention. He insinuates, and absconds when it suits him for the wilderness. This doctor who hauled me, an anchor of bone out of the soaked fathoms of fever, is transforming. He is becoming my patient, as much as I have been his. Turning on his toes like a dancing dog, he is suppliant to this shift. We are mostly bereft of medicines now. He says that he is loyal. Love and loyalty without limits are mere posturing. Nikolai Junker, false jester, Russian lapdog, shattered man—I should have killed him.

*One of the agents at Gibraltar, wearing a scarlet fez—smallpox bacillus—bullets—*Abandon, or set down the right form of man in the midst of the jungle and watch him, and compare him to others. It all returns to him. It comes back, you see? By his second or third night, some primeval requisite of night vision returns from its burial in the animal city of his bones. The temper of his senses alters. Secret nervures extend beyond him, ringing, tantalizing. The lucidity of deep eons asserts itself. You confessed once, My Intended, that after a glass of wine you felt the swim of a forgotten honesty, a loosening of words, senses prickling, distended, and sparkling. The right form of man receives this from the Congo. An exorbitant light floods his marrow. He becomes sensitive to every motion of foliage, each dry scuttle of insect legs, the rippling of centipedes, the rolling of mammals in the hot stew of their evening. The pitching of birds sets his hair erect. It is an erotic profusion that we have lost. Instinct has been circus-ringed with bricks, gaudy tenements of complacency. Life is a parody, under the rouge sunset of Gravesend, Grave-send, Grave's-end. The trained and mannered world is a tomb. Do you recall ever eating something powerfully sour? In your memory summon the sensation of eating lime, of your jaw where the sourness touched the ghost of your discarded gills, as if the slits might reopen just below your ears. I do not exaggerate to say that some phantom of this nature is ever-present—one is required merely to step back over the threshold of now. Junker does not have this. His garb mocks the kaleidoscopic forest, rather than becoming it. Do I contradict myself? I suppose that I must, living at the rim of things. Can I tell you that this place is scintillating with both beauty and corruption, and that I might report shades of torture for any bright bliss? When I return from my walk with the recoil of my rifle still stiff in my shoulder, a hippo gutted on the amber silt of a delta, or an elephant steaming from the holes of extracted tusks, is my death merely overdrawn with false light? Behold the émigré, the strange new king. The Russian irritates me. His mere existence here heckles me. Yet, survival is impossible if one can't live with bad taste.

I had a dream last night:

Sunrise, indigo to pink—I was standing erect within the eviscerated corpse of an elephant, the titanic gray sheath of its hide flowing out behind me, as I forced my head upward, through the smashed plates of the cranium, into the bloody hollow where the brain had been. All of the other bones had been stripped. The beast I wore splayed out in one giant cadaverous robe, as I became its spine, skull and operator. It was mine to work like an oriental under his paper dragon. Then, slowly, from some instinct, I pushed my hands, my forearms and then the full extent of my arms down into the tusks, until I was clad to my shoulders. As I strove to enter them, their weird marrow slopped out like blue clay. Strange mechanical sounds filtered in through the massive ears, a wet reverberation. I wanted to look out, but the eyes were set too far apart and the jellies were too dark and thick. Instead, I stared out from the hole in the brow, blown by my exploding bullet, engulfed in gore, the shifting of flies, and the awful fumes of putrescence. I tried to raise the tusks, so that I might advance toward the river. The water emitted its odd music. The effort of raising my arms in the hard shafts threatened to overwhelm me. I saw my own back ripping open under the great weight and my vertebrae spilling like white coins from the rented skin. At first, and for a long time, I was the only human tenant of my dream as I staggered forth in the too heavy flesh. I moved closer to the water. I said to myself, I suppose that it is the elephants, not the hyenas, becoming my conscience, impossible to bear. Through the large bullet hole, the sunlight was fierce. The day elapsed in sudden flashes, until, at dusk, I glimpsed the Station. It was burning. Flames and brilliant cinders rose into the darkening sky. The terrible epidermis dragged behind me, a leaden sheet painting a red stain across the earth. I thought, perhaps I could fill the trunk with water and put out the fire. Then, as I watched from the ragged makeshift eye, I saw that a boat was approaching along the channel. It was the mechanical sound that I had heard at the beginning. A steamer was coming slowly through the choked tributary to my Station. There was a white man standing in the bow. I saw him with the euphoria of a dying man who feels his pain suddenly eclipsed. The smoke from the fire must have cleared slightly, for he suddenly observed me. From within my vile costume, I tried to cry out to him, but suffocation prevented me. I realized further that I could recall none of the languages that I had ever spoken. I swung my collapsed head toward him, the impotent trunk trawling back between my legs as some satanic tail. I held my arms aloft, triumphantly encased in their white armor. A thin black figure stood beside the white man on the deck, raising a Winchester. I remember a spear arcing through the smoke. The white man on the steamer opened his mouth to scream—

Her breasts hang through corollas of beads as she struts the decrepit porch, passing like the shadowy ghost-blade of a sundial into my garden of skulls, my arcade of twisted ivory, and a dream that wakes me, rigid with fear. No, not yet.

Deplorable yellow houses—painted bricks—black tropics— Nsumbu, aspirant cannibal that he is, has developed a penchant for champagne, and since I am—beside the mad Russian—the only *white* here, it pleases me greatly to have him stop by, and for us to take our hygiene together. There was a half-caste here once, but I will postpone describing him until later. Nsumbu has appropriated the rat-ranked uniform of a dead Force Publique agent and has become quite urbane. That was disingenuous of me: the uniform that Nsumbu wears was once my own. I have not worn it in I do not know how long. From the moment that I first placed it upon him, Nsumbu adopted it. Kneeling on the wooden floor, we swig from the green magnums. Nsumbu rocks back and forth, the foam spilling from the corners of his mouth, as though permitting the waste of this finite thing is a subtle, unconscious insult. Then, he wipes his face with his sleeve and sucks the cuff dry. With the night comes a new perception, and my eyes dissolve the blue uniform and I witness his naked outline, the abdomen faceted and hard as a turtle shell, his arms of tar-dipped rope, and the wide respiring chest lifting and falling. Does he witness this of me? The mind is lonely. Slowly, the champagne washes me back to the region of my birth, or what I can recollect of it. My mother was a mongrel, as was my father. In the yellow book on my nightstand, the poet from my town says the same. The woman that you know as my mother is not my mother.

*Barges drift to the burning hospital—Albini rifles bayonet the abandoned sandbar—*I recall a Sunday morning on the Place Ducale, Charleville. Church was out, and Monsieur Prudhomme was on parade, still wearing his leather butcher's apron, the summer sun blading along his nose, and down the steak knife bayonet he had fixed to his militia rifle. It must have been 1878 or so. I was about thirteen years old. I regarded the butcher strutting in the pavilion shadows, making his quadrant, while flies sought out the gore of his business that stuck to his breast. Moist blackening from his beard painted his starched collar. His wooden shoes kept an amateur regimental time against the stones. I found that the window of his *boucherie*, just off the square on the Rue de Moulin, had been cracked. My mother had called it "a self-inflicted injury," which struck me because my father had recently said the same of me, as he punched me in the kidney. The crack in Monsieur Prudhomme's glass resembled a line of frozen lightning. Standing close, I saw the dangling meat through the fault in the glazing, now blurred and magnified—the hanging poultry, pheasants interrupted at disturbing angles twisted as they must have been by shot, the vivid livers and hearts illuminated by this concentration of crooked light. Later, I asked my mother why Monsieur Prudhomme would break his own window. Her knuckles were raw from laundering.

"He delivers false reports to the police. He's a provoca-teur, always looking for trouble."

"Don't they know he is lying?"

"Mais, oui," she shrugged. "Of course they do, Édouard. But they let him keep marching."

"La guerre contre la raison, contre fantômes et les ombres."

She did not hear me, and went on with her laundry, white suds drifting in the gloomy kitchen. I loitered, studying the way she fought on her scrubbing rack with the grass stains on my clothes. Outside the kitchen window, my father was going through his exercises. Finally, she looked up, exhausted. "Why are you so interested in him, anyway?"

"One day, I expect my shadow to revolt."

"You wouldn't know if it did."

"Wouldn't I?"

"Nah," she said, skeptical yet sympathetic, the Thames returning to her voice from years before. "Your shadow, like The Devil, would still stick to you like grease." My mother was descended from Cockneys. Most of her recollections of London were set in darkness, as though her life there had been nocturnal. For a long time, I thought she must have been a kind of explorer, with her illuminated streetwalking stories.

She met my father under gaslight, and was impressed by his accent and the floral shades of his bruises—a streetwalker and a journeyman—I never stood chance, did I? My father came from Ashkenazi Jews along the Rhine who spread north and outwards in veins of troubled blood. Sometimes, I would imagine that Monsieur Prudhomme could be my real father. There was something spectacular about him.

Stranglers on the plateau—acerbic clouds of teeth enwrap the dead—My father had been a professional bareknuckle fighter before I was conceived, and for a while after I was born, a stuttering career, of sorts. His engorged hands and ravaged features were testament to the hard fists of Europe. From Warsaw to the bear pits of Cologne, from the meadows of Flanders to the turf of Epsom racecourse, he had stuffed betting money and prizes into his rope belt. He worked for a time in Brussels for the printing firm Poot and Co., and I remember at another time for a vineyard to the southwest of us, when he would come home at weekends. This employment was always acquired accidentally, prior to or succeeding one of his fights, the intermittent stubborn bouts after I was born. Always, he would be fired after a short engagement, being light-fingered. From the storehouse of Joseph Krug he brought six bottles of champagne back to Charleville under his shabby pea coat. I recall the way he chimed, exhausted into our kitchen as my mother ironed clothes. Opening his coat where the contraband was bound to his body with knotted ropes, he announced, "If I ever set foot again in Reims, I'm a dead man!" He opened the first, sending the cork blasting across the room, clanging against one of the hanging saucepans. A volcano of white foam erupted onto the table as he hastened to pour it into whatever vessel came to hand. In 1873 or so, my first taste of champagne was from small teacup. I was eight years old. After a fight across the border in Charleroi, he went to Poot and Co. and did not return to us as often. He kept his job at Poot's for two months before he was discovered in the warehouse, long after midnight, prying open the petty cash box with an awl. He knocked out the night watchman and fled again. With only a few francs and a jaundiced volume of poetry stuffed into his pocket, my father returned to France. "I brought this back from Brussels for you Édouard, since you are a dreamer," he explained handing the book to me. He put the loose money on the kitchen table for my mother.

"I won't be going back, love," he said.

"Did you win your fight?"

"With Mertens? Of course I did. But the money . . ."

At some point between Brussels and getting home, my father had inscribed the book for me. I did not notice immediately, but on the final page he had scrawled the words "Little shit." It is with me, here in the sultry rook-black African night.

Acacias—marabou—carbolic acid—It was a cold near-Christmas dawn back in 1879 when they hung Prud-homme—seen too close as though I were a winter fly stalking between the stubble of his cheek. Terror reso-nated outward from his fat face, shimmering in the air like the tolling of an iron bell. Indeed, every inch of his flesh pumped out his fear, from the makeshift gallows and gibbet, and out over the dull crowd that had assembled on the Place Ducale to watch him dangle. I remember that he was dressed in a thin white gown that grew transparent in the wet of a light snowfall. The clean flakes settled and glim-mered upon the beam where the noose rope knotted. He seemed almost naked. Oily hair scrolled at his groin, and his belly pressed forth, heaving with his frightened breath. I

stared at his eyes, two sapphires dropped in a stopped wave
of tallow, the lids stiff with quiet agony. His tears dripped
upon his breast. His legs struggled to support him for a
few minutes longer. What crime had he committed? What
atrocity had dragged him here? Monsieur Prudhomme
appeared confused, unaware. I asked a woman, shivering
in the audience, what had he done? She shrugged. The neck
of Monsieur Prudhomme was the first that I ever saw, that
I ever heard, snapped by rope and drop. I don't remember
how the hangman looked, merely that some amorphous
shade worked there—a misty killer with his tackle. As he
put his rope over the crown of the butcher's snow-wet
head, the crowd behind me pushed forward, straining like
animals at their tethers, forcing me toward the gallows. I
feared that they might shove me beneath it. The trap swung
and Monsieur Prudhomme plummeted through the false
floor, his naked feet directly in front of my face, kicking
and jigging for what must have been merely a moment,
but which appeared to me a grotesque ballet reaching all
through Christmas and that New Year—his thick ankles,
his corkscrew toenails, and then the excrement running
down his pale calves. The next day, I suffered in my bed
with a terrible chill. My mother said that it was from the
shock, and from not dressing warmly enough.

I went out again and began my *dérive* through the sunlit
streets. Although I tried to become lost, I found myself,
invariably, at the watermill on the great coil of la Meuse,
encountered a short walk north of the square, beyond the
butcher's broken window where the Rue de Moulin meets
the quayside. It was tall, a powerful block constructed over
several arches through which the millrace flowed. It was
the zenith of the day and my shadow cleaved close. I knew
that I was not the first to experience the old ramparts of

Charleville as the grey confines of a cancerous cell. Feeling my sunburn on the quayside, I recall slowly becoming aware of a second shadow beside my own, and almost unconsciously, I looked down over my hip. A black, long-muzzled dog with a dense coat had followed me along the Rue de Moulin and now attended me as I contemplated the mill. The stray whined with thirst and I showed a place where it could drink. Its eyes were the color of mahogany, and as it breathed I caught a glimpse of its sharp white teeth.

Nsumbu is lying in the shivering grass. She is scowling, threading fangs back onto her damaged necklace. I pour myself a large Gordon's and drink it in a single tilt. Not yet.

*Tinned butter—dead crocodile arranged on the glossy piano— sarcophagus—*Outside my barrack, across the dark of a plain muted by rainfall, I think I can hear the melancholy rasp of elephants. How many more of them can there be? Elephants are gravity and grave. Each resembles a tract of mud wrenched up from the earth by an invisible hand and momentarily suspended, filth and tentacle drooling down, back to earth. Existence, for elephants, is the inexorable sucking of the mud, hauling them back inside that slick, penumbral murk whence they came—the elongation of the trunk groping low, the collapsing orbits of their giant skulls as they negotiate one another in the dusk, their flat unshaped feet never distinct from the dirt. To encounter them in their slurry, half submerged in viscid brown water, is to witness one of God's mighty aberrations seeking return to its inevitable element. One hears them, singing back to subterranea, their apocalypse of stone. The elephant is Jehovah's clay Golem tearing its ghetto of trees—it is the white rib of Adam still protruding from a wanton and terrible woman, the tusk! What other ivory could cut that umbilicus of gumbo out of the groves and set them pitching through the night? I can see them now, sounding the black oratory of their extinction, gray leather ragged with flak, and dripping in monsoons, all persistence and endurance eroded. Across the great blades of ice that carved our continent these mammoths swung and lumbered, there in the snow before London under a parliament of crows—there in the gilded saddles of the Alps where Hannibal, the Carthaginian, descended on Rome, in the bone char vortex of Turner's painting—there in the prehistory of mangroves, in the filmy lagoons of malaria, they have been there, rolling stubbornly to death. To watch them barging in the dawn, the misshapen sun roiling the grass, is to behold the butting of flesh against the limits of time. Boom! Boom! Boom! It strikes me, now, that Nsumbu, Monsieur Prudhomme and I are the same, in our absurd, bloody uniforms, delivering our false reports. False reports? No, this is the one true report of my station and my ideas.

The *Chien de Berger Belge,* my black dog shadow from beneath the watermill, I named Leo, and I resolved to take him to London with me when it was time to bury my mother. The year was 1881, early October. I was not quite sixteen. With Leo and my mother's casket, we were to journey by paddle steamer from Calais to Dover. My father and I took her coffin by locomotive to Calais, and then to the dockside upon a two-wheeled cart. There, my father abandoned us. He had been waiting for his chance to leave France for Belgium, and then to Germany and Poland. "It had to be," he said, stroking rainwater from the glossed lid. "A tumor the size of a cabbage. I don't think she ever recovered from having you cut out of her, poor bitch." She died suddenly of a hemorrhage. My father tried to whitewash the floorboards afterwards, but the paint seemed to draw out slivers of blood, oxidizing but not yet dried, leaving the kitchen smeared pink and brown-black. E is black. Édouard that she often pronounced Edward like a Cockney is black—inconsolable, the negritude of my grief rose up with the sea walls of the harbor. What was it that Matthew Arnold said? *O that, to share this famous scene, I saw, upon the open sand, Thy lovely presence at my side, Thy shawl, thy look, thy smile, thy hand!*

Before my father turned away from us, I recall momentarily that he squinted out across the English Channel, his face smashed by grief. Fleetingly, something of jellied eels, pearls and barges passed over him. My mother's dying wish was to be sent to London, to be buried with her ancestors. Now, without my mother, he would take his last opportunity to return to the east. His sorrow, but also his release from the boredom of Charleville, and from the self-inflicted wound, me, turned him toward the Prussian Partition and the Tenth Pavilion of the Warsaw Citadel. Within the proximity of death, people become sentimental and stupid. He would go back to his ancestors and die hence. I saw a single tear drip from a bloodshot eye before the remnants of his spirit were whipped from him by a salted wind. He deserted us so silently that I almost did not realize that he was gone. I lowered the front of the cart, my mother's dead feet close to the paving.

That house, cold as a salt block, the brick dust on my shoulders where I would lean against my bedroom wall, staring through the window toward the Belgian border, a dead elm clawing the horizon—the haunted floorboards where my father's boots hammered and scraped through old boxing drills—my mother's eyes squinting through the frost on the windowpanes, imagining that I had run away again. I would try to reach Paris, or the border, hobbling exhaustedly in filthy lanes, cutting across dewy fields, sleeping rough and waking stiff in the sparkling fog of hunger. Was it that I truly hated my home? I don't know. The crenellated city walls were evidence of some nobility, some aristocracy that would forever exclude me. I would try to run away to other cities to discover if they were all inscrutable, impenetrable and lonely. Returned or forced home, my mother would weep over me, and my father, in his relief, would whip me with his belt. They would ask, were they not good enough for me? How could I explain that I wasn't certain? How could I tell them that perhaps I wanted no one?

When I recall him, I see fists and flannel. I see him in the noon sunlight, in the small yard outside the kitchen door, jabbing his hard knuckles toward ghostly opponents, wheeling around him, the material of his navy trousers slapping in the thin breeze as he weaves through his exercises, penetrating some invisible defense. I can hear the terse and sibilant exhalation as he lets his punches go, a noise that makes me think of the blackness of galaxies ripping, letting in little steam jets of despair from somewhere behind their walls. His compressed breath shocks the air before him and he pivots his soft shoes in the gravel. The sun reddens his shoulders, and his nostrils flare behind the blur of his blood-filled hands. From where I am watching, in my memories, his moustache gleams wet with sweat and saliva. The triangle formed by his trapezius and bald head sways like a cobra's hood. Sometimes, he would hold up his open palms before me, and order me to strike them until my bones hurt and my small fingers trembled. At other times, he would bark at me to punch for his ribs, but I could never reach him. He skipped weightlessly away from me as I lost my breath. These drills he performed to intimidate my mother. She watched him through the kitchen window above the basin as she washed laundry there. It would seem to me, at first, that he was simply watching himself move, reflected in the glass pane. If I changed my attitude slightly, I could see through his reflection to my mother inside, looking out. Finally, I saw her flinching, and I comprehended the ritual between them. He would remove his dirty shirt, and she would soap and scrub the collar until her hands were raw, staring out, while he glared inward, throwing casting blows at the woman behind his reflection. It was a peculiar torture.

I recall my father staring at the pale planes of my face. As we ate our meals at table, I could feel his scrutiny, his cold eyes scraping at me. His gaze ran over me, silent, salacious, sculpting, watching for the first stubble of my puberty. The morning that he saw it, he could barely finish his breakfast. His right hand twitched upon the white tablecloth when he saw me test the hair barely emerging from my jaw, gently rasping under my fingernails. I sipped the last coffee from my china bowl. As I rose, excusing myself, my father gripped my wrist. He told me to wait. He needed to demonstrate something.

Upstairs, he lathered my face—birdsong beyond the cracked bathroom windowpanes. He stood behind me, holding the razor. It passed before my eyes, the luminous blade making hypnotic angles and tilts, crossing before me like the gleaming side of a ship. "Don't rush," he said, "get the pressure right." His voice was low, sonorous. Although he held the razor, he spoke as if his hand was mine. With his left hand, he raised my chin, holding it between his scissor fingers. "*There,*" he said. I didn't feel the blade making its incision, but he had slit the skin of my throat with one subtle push. Painlessly, a three- or four-inch sliver of blood, hair thin, developed there. "You might as well know what it's like." I saw him in the mirror, the involuntary lick of his lips. Purposefully, he had cut me. Time stopped. We were absolutely still. A bird sang before he wiped the bloody metal in the warm basin—my mother's blood turning black.

Very ill—phenacetin powder—whisky sour ... The paddle steamer came in through the remnants of a storm, her twin funnels piercing the gauze of rain, letting out their smoke. I thought the steamer would come to the dockside, but she stopped short, and as hours elapsed small rowing boats went out and slowly unloaded the passengers who swarmed as ants along a knife blade. I watched the steamer pitching in the sea, and leaned against the coffin on its small wooden cart. My dog leaned against my leg. I turned to look behind me, for a glimpse of my father, but he was gone. There was nothing left, but to try to push the cart to the tideline where I might manage to load us into one of the sculling boats. There was a stone ramp down to the beach. For some time, I merely stared out over the beach from this promontory of the French coast, the slipway with its clinging brown weed at the edge of my sight. In those moments, I could think of nothing more cruel than a ferry of the dead that would anchor itself so many fathoms out, or the mockery of a gale that would prevent it from coming in for the mourners and the mourned, marooned on the cold stone of their pasts. Given the futility of the task, I admit some reluctance in taking up the funereal cart again.

It threatened to pull away from me as I descended the ramp to the shingle that had washed up around it. Something ripped beneath the skin of my shoulders. No sooner had the cart touched the edge of the beach than its wheel rims sunk into the shingle. It would not move, no matter how I strained against it. The sea gleamed, impossibly distant, yet probably only a few minutes of ordinary walking. I looked about for anyone that might help me. Two young women assisted an elderly gentleman down to the beach, all of them laughing as he shuffled on the brown weed. They passed me by and continued unimpeded toward the firmer wet sand closer to the waves. I watched them being helped into a sculling boat by a sailor who began to row them to the steamer. A pale ribbon was stripped from one of the women by the Channel breeze, and then the sun flowed over me, prickling sweat from my brow. Leo lay at my feet. Another man, well dressed, shifted his tall hat at the sight of the coffin, but hurried past. Despairing of the cart, I took out my knife and began to slice at the ropes that held the coffin in place. I took the rope handles in my hands and hauled it off, onto the shore. But as I did so, one of the ropes snapped, burning my palm as my grip tore away. Finally, I stood the vessel upright, embracing it, and wrestling it an inch above the beach. Then, I was able to stagger backwards with it toward the ferry. Leo barked and looped about me, as though the dark dog was my master, forcing me beyond my limits. Splinters sewed my hands to the wood, and I heard my mother's corpse booming inside from the jolts of my reversed wrestler's gait. Several times, I almost fell, the burden pushing the air from my lungs. As I passed from the shingle to the wet sand, I fought with the wretched image of my mother's face, separated from mine by a pauper's layer of coffin plank, lolling grotesquely, blue and beating almost against me, though she had no blood left to bruise with. Her odor worked through the backbreaking door, as I embraced her death.

Le sort du fils de famille, cercueil prématuré couvert de limpides larmes.

"Bloody hell, mate!" At last, a sailor materialized at my side. "Let me help you, for God's sake." As he took up the low end of the casket, and I was able to lower the weight from my chest, I saw that he was wearing a uniform of navy blue, with a yellow star upon his cap. It was only as we reached the boats and I felt the sea wash over my ankles that I had the breath to thank him, and I then understood that he was not part of the steamer crew.

"You're not employed by the South Coast Railway?" I said.

"The London and Brighton owns this ship, all right, but I work for no man, anymore."

"Your uniform?"

"Says I work for the Company in Kinshasa, off Stanley Pool, but God's truth, every man down *there* works for his self." A cloud passed before the sun, and I regarded the deep shade of his skin, the emaciation of his face, and the unnatural whiteness of his short hair. "It got me out of the gutter, but blokes are dropping like flies from blue jack, so you reap and half-inch what you can get for yourself, and then get out bloody quick." Abruptly, at his own invocation of disease, I saw his compassion evaporate as he eyed the casket with the superstitious caution of a man who knows he has ridden his luck to ground, and finds he is vulnerable. It was as if he was waiting for a moment of arbitrary cruelty to catch up with him. Later, I would learn that *blue jack* meant cholera. "You don't mind me asking," he began.

"C'est ma mère," I said. "Il n'est pas contagieux. Not contagious. She wanted to be buried in England. She was more English than French." It seemed absurd to me, explaining. As he inclined his head, examining the broken rope handle, I saw him haloed by the sun. I said: "One plot is like another, in the end, I suppose."

"No. No, you're wrong. It's more than dirt, ain't it, really? Much more than dirt. It has to be."

I looked back up the beach, at my deep footprints, scrapes where I had almost let her fall, and to the abandoned cart.

"If it's all the same dirt, then why would I bother getting

back to Chatham?" He said this while searching his pockets for tobacco.

I shrugged.

He lowered his voice, speaking through his teeth as he lit a carved white pipe. "Believe me, I've seen it." The foaming salt water lapped against us. When the next rowing boat came in, he helped me gather the coffin again, and with a London to Brighton oarsman, we bore my mother's corpse into the low waves. I lifted Leo into the boat and we were ferried out of the shallows. The dog seemed not to mind it. About me, I saw the activity increase, with more diminutive vessels shuttling between the steamer and the shallows. Handing me his pipe, he flicked his head back: "What's your name, mate?"

"Edward. Edward Kurtz."

"Yid?"

"I don't think I'm anything." As I put the ivory between my lips, I caught an abstract scent of gunpowder, and something made me say, "Yet."

His name was Eric Paine.

We came alongside the paddle steamer, the blue iron hull rising and bulging over us as we shunted against it. The oarsman yelled to his comrades, who dropped ropes for us to fasten the casket. Then we were hauled up. The oarsman spoke as we rose, swaying and clanging against the superstructure. "Once we get going, we'll make close to twenty knots, if the chop isn't too bad. We should see the White Cliffs after about an hour. We'll see how it is to get in. Hopefully, we won't have to run down to Folkestone. Get in as intended, weather permitting." Paine sucked hard on the brined air. "Nearly home, boys."

On the deck, we stood with the coffin between us. We made a queer scene: the mourning boy, his dog, and casket, with the white-haired man, aching for his hometown. Two porters agreed to stow the coffin, more out of deference to the sensibilities and superstitions of the other passengers than of sympathy for my baffled sorrow, I think. I learned that Paine had been in Africa for six months. He unfolded for me a crushed pocket map illustrating the serpentine river where he had been, pointing out marks and stations that, though they meant nothing to me, he invested with sublimity, the reverence one has for places haunted by almost visceral memories. As though it were burning, his long fingers shifted the disintegrating paper. Then, he handed it to me, this limp, indecipherable sheet. But, surely, he would want to keep it? He had memories enough, he explained, and he would never again return to the downcast continent where he had made his luck. He considered himself uncannily fortunate to have survived his station. As we walked the deck of the paddle steamer, he evoked the stripped canopies, the dynamite and quinine, the laudanum, and the explosive rifle rounds, the prodigious elephants and their ivory.

"Six months, man. That's all it took to transform me from beggar to baron." He ran his fingers through his pale hair. "Granted, lost me some fat, scorched my skin, had a few obscene dreams—there's nothing like the solitude of a pallet under fever."

"What did you do before, did you mean that you were a beggar?"

"Nah, not a beggar, but near as damn it. I was a bargeman, ferrying coal on the canals, but that's dead work—canals are almost at their end in England. I used to be black with coal, listening to my voice echoing under the stone bridges. But, where I've been, I felt like I was the only white man for miles, speaking English under that bloody steaming sky. Listen, I say that a working man is more ready to endure out there, he that has known a scraped knuckle or three, a little vomit from cheap gin, a bit of hardship. After a life in the shit in the city, then a nice glass of claret after whipping a tardy nigger ain't so bad, is it?" He saw me flinch. "What now?" he laughed, incredulous. "Oh, you'd do it, I can tell you. Someone like you, who knows no luxury, suddenly finds it in a gimmick. You should have seen yourself on the beach. You might as well be pushing your own coffin to London, son."

I turned away from him, resting my palms on the wooden guardrail, staring at the slate-gray water. Leo, his ebony coat glossed with sea spray, lay upon the deck. I moved my shin against him, seeking some reassurance. Paine went on, his voice tempered.

"Forgive me for being blunt. That's the thing. If a white man, specially one from my class, *your* class, could live in the jungle long enough, he could forget that he ever experienced any kind of servitude, no slings and arrows, although there are arrows enough in the jungle. But, *in there*, his class is washed from him. He finds himself raised up, if he just keeps breathing. He finds a hundred hours in a minute. His repose and sleep are justified. His lusts are sated. His thirst is slaked. Take me, who used to resemble nothing so much as the coal I carried. Now, I'm an ivory man, a *retired* ivory man with medals and money to boot, enough to coast all my days through. I made it serve me, and I got *out*." He spat the word with a determined violence. I think that he felt the eyes of some of the other promenading groups turn toward him. Suddenly self-conscious, he ducked toward the rail to stand close beside me before he spoke again. His voice, a harsh stage whisper, barely survived the afterward slap of the paddles and the hiss of the brined breeze. "I got out." He repeated his words. Perhaps he was convincing himself of their accuracy. He saw that I was still holding the decaying map of his life. He smiled as he took it back from me. I remember the manner in which he pinched it by one corner between his fingers, holding it up into the wind, watching it flap. Then, it was gone. "I acquired tastes," he said. "I educated myself. And the mind is its own place, they say, and in itself can make a heav'n of hell and a hell of heav'n."

Eric Paine took strange delight in his African transformation. Had he a mirror, he would have addressed it—without a mirror, he addressed me. I confess that he was, indeed, mesmerizing, in ways that reminded me of Monsieur Prudhomme, the butcher of Charleville, or even my father. Now, with the passing of years, there is, for me, nothing unexpected in encountering a man for who certain of the mainstays of sanity have unraveled. Repetition has inured me to the broken porcelain of other men's minds. Still, there, under the blue iron funnels of the ship, swarming with modern people bound for Dover, it struck me that these men, Prudhomme and Paine, would increase their kind. That vivid man-eating wilderness inside the skull was spilling out into all our cities. Paine was wrong in one sense, at least: the solitude of fever is with all of us—each of us has his incommunicable disease that can be transmitted neither by blood nor word. Paine was not truly modern. If he were, then he would have remained in Africa.

The White Cliffs of Dover, bone yard pale, rose sheer and coruscating in the sunlight, and the name of the land never sounded so English as it did when I breathed it French: *Ah, Anglaterre*, my mother's body. *Ma mere, la mer, merde*, I saw the land splitting, carbon-black mammoths falling from the serrated plateau, dashed on chalky rocks, brown elephants bursting their entrails into the low tide, species after incumbent species shorn by the precipice.

Insidiously, Eric Paine had suggested it to me. He asked, who was the man he had seen me with, on the beach, my father? He had seen his indifferent shrug as he turned from us. He asked if my mother's name was on the coffin. If I did not disembark with her, my mother's body would surely, eventually, be unloaded on the French side. Then, would it not follow my father wherever he went? "You couldn't possibly make it, son. It must be eighty miles to London. Fancy him abandoning you on the beach like that," he said. "Let her haunt him," he said.

Even as the Company man spoke to me, a blue-uniformed Satan with his yellow star flashing from his peaked cap in the blazing Channel—how can I explain it?—a black stripe fell horizontally across my vision, between us. It dropped so quickly that I flinched, as though part of the ship's rig had detached and crashed onto the deck. But Paine did not react. He went on talking about what was right and revenge. The steamer ploughed on for Admiralty Pier, the stone spur dog-legging out below the primordial whitewash of the cliff face. I rubbed my eyes with my knuckles. There was a wicked stiletto pain in the sockets. Sea gulls flocked over the funnels, a white blur of wings. As Paine removed his Company cap, breathing on and polishing his star with sleeve, I felt nausea uncurling from the base of my skull, dilating into my chest. He was saying something that I could not understand. As I watched his lips shaping the dumb words, I realized that the gulls gliding above our wash made no sound. The steamer throbbed beneath my feet, yet the ship and the sea had become part of the surface of a terrifying silence. A second stripe fell, a shadowy whip that I heard cracking between my eyes. Paine's expression shifted, registering whatever stricken aspect was visible in me. He reached toward me with both hands. I saw his cap spin to the deck and roll beneath the iron railings into the sea between the hull and the pier. Black stripes cascaded through my line of sight—broken Venetian blinds—darkness exploded around me in one immense convulsion—

Moko Jumbi poling through the Atlantic waves—smoking hemp cheroot—grinning—I didn't know how I left the ship. I awoke in a filthy, shambolic street, with my spine against a crumbling red brick wall. My memories remained slivers, glimpses of consciousness, and attenuated strips of being. The pain in my eyes had lapsed, but I was lost. I knew that I must be in Dover. Trembling with indescribable sorrow, I got to my feet and staggered through the constricted alleys, following the slope of the cobbles and the outcry of the sea and ships' horns. When I encountered a person, I tried to say what I wanted: "La jétee? La jétee?" At last, finding my way back to Admiralty Pier, I discovered that the steamer had gone, returning to Calais. I walked out along the promontory, blubbing through the small groups of passengers waiting for the next ferry, still believing that I might find my mother's casket and my dog waiting patiently beside it on the wet stones, if only I went out far enough. There was nothing.

They found me on Shakespeare Cliff, leering out over the granite sea, my legs dangling over the edge where I sat. At this chalky precipice, hundreds of feet above the narrow flint line of the beach, I remember ripping out handfuls of the damp grass. I would toss it about me, testing the wind, watching the blades blow away over the water. I kicked my heels against the white rocks, loosening small fragments and dust. I knew that, in time, I would succeed in kicking the delicate ledge from beneath my body and I would fall to the rocks below. I heard voices at my back. Two fishermen had seen me there. I ignored them and continued kicking at the cliff face, harder, leaning over and watching the crumbling stone. I suppose I must have appeared like a petulant child on a swing. My heels were bloody. I flexed my elbows, ready to push myself off if they came too close. I closed my eyes, and listened. Just as I caught the smell of their oil coats, I cried out and shoved myself forward. I was too slow. They hauled me, struggling, away from the ledge, pulling me through the grass. I remember the white and yellow of the daisies.

*Kwanga paste—leaves in mortar—yams under silver machete—*I was at Broadmoor for a long time. It was an imposing mansion for criminals and the insane, although, in truth, beyond the red brick portcullis it was a serene place, for the greater part—stately wings built on a hillside surrounded by oak trees, rookeries, foxglove and rippling bluebells. The inmates were more melancholic than criminal, playing slow games of cricket on the lawns, tending the bright gardens of roses and snapdragons. There were many fascinating specimens of men and women inside. They admitted a poet named McLean who had tried to kill Queen Victoria. He had it right. I listened to the dialects floating over the croquet mallets and the tin dinner plates until I could ventriloquize any one of them, and assume any convenient cant. With my English mother and my wandering Jewish father, I reasoned that I would never have but one voice, but I wanted to fit in. So, to the Cockneys, I was Bow Bells, pearls and jellied eels, a rag and bone shadow, I was Thames water and adenoidal couplets suspended in the air of Drury Lane. To the Scousers, I was scouse, the flat reedy cormorant tones of any other prowler of the Mersey mudflats, looking westward to Ireland. To the Black Countryman, I was thick as a pit, coal in my lungs. To the Welshman, I was lyrical as the singing by the Cardiff Arms Park, the rolling ratchet of turnstiles and foaming pints of beer. The Glaswegian taught me to lament at speed, and the Yorkshireman stoicism in drear cogs of wind and rain. There were more. I went easily among them all and had lost almost all of my French tones. Within the library at Broadmoor, I worked on my ideas, devouring all that I could—the Metaphysical Poets, Livy, Blake, Tacitus, Marx, Baudelaire, Byron, Shelley, *The Feast of Blood,* about the vampire who casts himself into a volcano, and Darwin, of course—*runners whom renown outran, and the name died before the man*—I wrote poems there, also. Institutionalized, secretive, one learns how to write in miniscule, ant-legged script, like this. Any man who spends time in prison or an asylum learns to fill precious paper with as many of his ideas as he can compress there. He becomes intimate with almost childish ambitions, and the most curious difficult of notions about himself. Sometimes, a bricked-up shorthand evolves, like a man of Fleet Street recording murders in pocketbook. Memories and ideas are set down in scraps, rolled into cracks in the walls, pressed under the insole of shoes.

The man in the next dormitory was a murderer named Dadd. His tubercular hacking made an insomniac of me for the years that I was there, but I confess that I enjoyed him and would not have wished it another way. I thrived in his conversation about the desolation of Egypt and in watching him work at his easel, painting spectral canvasses. Dadd had slashed his father's throat with a razor and taken the next ferry from Dover to Calais. We were not that far apart in our parricidal impulses. Dadd had been living at Broadmoor for seventeen years when we met, and in Bedlam for the score before, after Montreau and Fontainebleu. Madness brings out the cosmopolitan in one. His tarry beard was streaked with gray, and his eyes were blown bulbs of shattered glass. The stroke of insanity had traced his brow as he lay in the prow of a barge on the River Nile. The finger of his fever stopped between his brows and began an insistent drilling, and through that cavity the intonations of ancient gods had proceeded. They bored in, warning him, encouraging him, and instructing him in the mysteries of Osiris. Even as he painted in the room next to mine, a version of his body was still out there, reddening on the deck of a boat on that river. His shell was in a corner of England, coughing over his oils. When he held his brush horizontally, calculating some perspective, measuring the height of one of his spirits, it cut the air as his blade must have that autumn in Cobham. "Imagine yourself, Kurtz," he said, "betrayed, and shut in an iron maiden, cut to pieces and cast into the Nile in ribbons . . ."

I thought then, in my sanatorium, how valuable it is to live to the contrary: that a man's name be immeasurable, louche, uncontainable, infinite even as his body turns to the common dust. When a page of some book struck me, I would rip it from its bindings and fix it to the wall of my narrow room. For adhesive I used porridge, and sometimes my own mucous. There is, perhaps, nothing more difficult on this earth for a Charleville runt stuck in a Berkshire asylum to conceive, but it came to me like an instinct to swim against the bad flow of all my blood and to live as man and ghost, auspice and omen, to divine my royal ambivalence. Dadd told me: "Every nation's ruin comes to it from its rivers."

*Jiggers hatch between atrophied toes—sewing needles—bathing—*With Dadd's advice, I taught myself to paint at Broadmoor. I began with sketching on my bed sheets, an almost unconscious vandalism that got me noticed. I was trying to draw a picture of my father, and a portrait of myself beside him, to make some comparison and divine something of my nature. Far from being punished, I was encouraged and provided with watercolors to discover *en plein air* while the lunatics swung their croquet mallets and crows flew from the copse and over the red wards. The tranquility of the madhouse held time in place. I stopped counting the days, as I had when I was first confined. I felt then that the trailing blank of my life was catching up with me, and the voids of misery were filling in with a new being. The alchemy of oil paints, I learned painstakingly, drunk with turpentine, my shoes spattered. I set up before a mirror in my narrow room and worked on a self-portrait. The face upon the tacky canvas was always someone else's. I have to wonder if the face that I was painting then is the face that hangs on me now.

The hypnotist at Broadmoor was named MacIntyre. He was an angular figure in gray tweeds, sitting awkwardly in a small leather chair. I met him after being inside for three months. His voice was soft, and he spoke as though he were himself sedated, a slow almost drawling Edinburgh affect. He had a few pages of notes resting in his lap.

"I like a man who can keep time," MacIntyre said, rising to shake my hand. "I've been looking over your records. No more seizures since the second week after you arrived. That's good. Do you recall anything of that episode?"

I sat down in another leather chair across the desk from him. He offered me a cigarette that I accepted and lit before saying anything else. "I was washing my face, and I saw the stripes again, like blinds coming down. It happened very quickly, I think."

"Do you remember what you might have had on your mind, that morning?"

I remembered very clearly. "Yes."

"How old are you, Edward?"

"Almost seventeen."

"Can you tell me what you were thinking as you washed your face?"

"My father killed my mother."

We sat in silence.

Finally, MacIntyre picked up a white fountain pen. He held it close to my eyes so that it I had to strain to focus upon it. "What we're going to do will not hurt you. I'm going to encourage you, gently, to remember . . ."

I dreamed of Eric Paine.

I will never forget the perverse grin he cast at me when we disembarked, leaving the casket and my mother's corpse behind—or the way he vanished like a phantom into the crowds on the English dockside. However irrational the notion, I was certain that I would encounter him again. As I recollect it now, I can see the banking of the seagulls over the funnels of the paddle steamer, and I know that I was imagining the body of my mother, endlessly, pointlessly ferrying between Dover and Calais. How much time would pass, I asked myself, before she would be discovered, half-Cockney, decomposing, suspended on the sea? The casket was unmarked—her body bore no identification. My father had pawned her meager jewelry. Stranded in the shipping lane, down in the iron hull, she would pass back and forth, accumulating superstitions. The family had disintegrated. As I grinned, walking away as my father had done before me, abandoning the dead, I felt my lips conform to the mask of Eric Paine. I suffered a flicker of disgust. Yet, was it disgust at myself, that hyena smirk, or the shadow of a callous sun? I will not say. That flash of abjection showed me the hard edges and limits of reality, and the seduction of oblivion. And I resolved that a man must be as ruthless with his time as time is with him. My black dog refused to leave the steamer. My final image is of him lying beside my mother's coffin, below deck, his jaw resting on the metal floor. Yet more than anything else, trapped in my crucible inside Broadmoor, I had years to recall the vision of Eric Paine holding up his decaying map of the territories and tributaries of Africa in the breeze as we crossed the English Channel. I would see it flying from his fingers, ripping to shreds, the tiny fragments sucked into the sea.

It haunted me.

Manioc leaves—clay—monstrous fish with fangs—chimpanzee paw—There was a warden at Broadmoor named Fordham, a thickly set man with a soiled beard. He was missing one of his front teeth and his lips and fingers were yellow with smoking. Sometimes, he would slip a woodbine to me and we would smoke together. One day, very close to the end, I asked him if it would be possible to procure me a book, any book, about Africa. Two days later, he brought me his own edition of *King Solomon's Mines*. It struck me as a foolish yarn, but I never told him that I found it so. Fordham was very proud of his perception that one of the maps could be turned over to look like the anatomy of a woman. He spoke of it on more than one occasion, the *mouth of the treasure cave* leading to *the pit* and the fallopian *idols*. Then there were the mounds of *Sheba's breasts* and the mountain ranges extending like arms away from these. Fordham told me that he hoped this would assuage my melancholy, and that it might help me understand whatever symbols I had seen under MacIntyre's hypnosis. Yet, the true light was Paine's map. He had gone out there an insect and returned a spider.

It was fixed within me long before the day that you and I met. How could you compare with that fateful luminescence coming at me from the night? It is cruel, too cruel. You had no chance—not against the phosphorescent white lure of that lost map flickering inside my skull. As the sea shifted through seasons beneath my wire bed, disembodied I went after the erotic cartographies of my future. There was not a day that I spent inside that I did not whip my memories after it, pushing my senses to reclaim it, to remember. At first, I sought to scratch the spirals of the river upon the uneven walls of my cell with a loosened nail. In sleep, the cold, salt wind of that Calais morning would blow over me. Later, when I had chalk, I would illustrate the cement floor with impressions of Africa that were, almost certainly, imaginary. My skin felt shocks at its absence. Remorse rippled through me when I remembered the map passing back from my fingers into Eric Paine's. I could feel his ivory tobacco pipe in my mouth. I could still envisage his blue uniform on the steamer deck.

Coma victim floating off starboard—tamarind—stone piers— Nsumbu has passed out from the champagne. In a few minutes, I will drag his unconscious frame outside and leave him propped against my doorframe beneath this deep African sky. Another belt of rain will pass over us. This is one of our rituals: my putting him out of the house like an incontinent dog, though, I love him. He is as heavy as soddened rope. I have worked my best to educate him and we share some words of a common tongue, some English, some of his native language, and some of the idiomatic grunts and hand gestures that men may make between one another that in time prove comprehensible, even to the savage. I wear one language like another. By the time I arrived in London, I could shrug the cobwebs of French from my shoulders and go about like an Englishman. You should hear Nsumbu recite "The Tyger"—all phonetic bass and strange: "Een duh four rests odah nite."

Early morning, brick dust and gruel white—From the melancholy hill and red wards and wings of Broadmoor, I emerged free of seizures after four years. Fordham gave me some money, enough for a train fair and a night in a hostel. He was a good man. From the asylum, I went to London. Riding the train, with my head leaning against the third class glass, I imagined how things might have been in 1881 when the gravediggers kept their appointment, and dug a slick trench during a downpour, expecting me, and my mother who would never arrive. I can still see them, loitering beside their wet excavation, regarded through the dismal cemetery gates with those stupid wreaths. The train steamed through a mirage of Home Counties doubt and rain. The glue of an old skin is not so easily cast off. Strange, also, to remember London, squatting here where the canopy of the jungle has been blasted away, cut and stripped for this station at the end of the world. When I arrived at Piccadilly, the station was ribbed with iron, smoking and loud. Hundreds of people crammed along the platforms. Flower sellers crouched, and newspaper sellers cried out headlines that echoed under the dirty roof.

I tarried that first morning in the winter of 1885 upon the Thames embankment. The sulfurous yellow haze had dispersed after a gale, revealing the city in its terrible clarity, and all of its lineaments forced themselves against my face. The unobstructed light flashed hard off the hulls, and the sharp boats interrupted the brown water. I had heard so much about London and its gauzy gray atmosphere that I remember some disappointment at the clean air, the crystalline day. The balustrades were stark, and dockside cranes made incisions against the vivid blue sky. I had imagined the parliamentary clock would sound through a baffle of mist, all reflections through a cataract of rain. The green streaks in the pigeon feathers electrified me. The tolling of the time came like a cannon shot through empty air. Dumb luck, I told myself. On another day it might be seen precisely as I had desired it, that brown opiated slop, that vortex of soot and the odd fur of a landscape jealous of its own mystery. It was as if having escaped paralyzing hysteria, I wanted to confront it in the external world, to see the city as it were in its bleakest aspect.

*Whitewashed faces—my litter carried through tall grass— brachiaria ruziziensis—*The woman whom you have known as my mother is not Mrs. Kurtz, but Mrs. Albert. I was her lodger. She was my landlady. Ours is a world of surrogates—*J'ai vécu partout. Pas une famille d'Europe que je ne connaisse—*We lived near the tannery at what she called "the better end" of Jamaica Road. It was there that I went to work in the drying room. I carried the heavy sheets of animal hide through the hot factory air to the racks, where it hung for a week or more. I was Mrs. Albert's only tenant. The windowpanes of her tenement were always caked with soot, and the red bricks smothered by it, so that the place was nearly invisible. The knocker at the front door was a brass lion, and she was exceedingly proud of it. When I met her, she was as poor as an insect, and not the way you know her now, after I came into some money. I want her left out of it. I remember that she loved gin and lemon. You only knew her later, from teahouses in the West End and slow perambulations of Regents' Park. You never saw where we had lived.

*Bleak smoke from the copper mines—mire crabs—*Perhaps one man could be regarded as being responsible for my education. I encountered him toward the close of 1888. I walked the dirty old river to Southwark. There I found him, wreathed in cigarette smoke, inside the George Inn. I had sought a seat at any table in vain, and became jammed close to his in a standing crowd of drinkers, all resembling one anemone, its blue, gray and black tendrils swaying in a turbid current of noise. Men, agitated and intoxicated, leaned against one another, drips of milk stout patterning their white shirts. Some had tweed caps balanced in the crook of their arm, and one had an apron of dried blood. The man at the table beside my hip had around forty years behind him, and he was dressed in a charcoal gabardine suit. He wore about his neck a red cravat, the frayed ends of which hung over his cream shirt. His fingers were brown from cigarettes. A cloth cap was pitched back on his head so that it appeared as if were about to slip from his scalp. Prematurely gray hair, heavy with oil, pushed out from beneath it. His complexion was lightly pockmarked, and he possessed strange gray eyes that would become blue or green in certain lights. Occasionally gasping on his woodbine, he was having a conversation with a lithe young man at his table.

"I suppose you never saw Perrot dance, cause you're too young."

The young man at the table shook his head and sipped nervously at his beer, his lips almost missing the rim of the glass. He was smartly dressed, and appeared out of his element.

"Jules Perrot would have made a marvelous burglar!" The man thumped the table with his stained fist, cocking his head toward the high corner of the room, as though cussing some imagined agency. Beneath the red cravat, the collar of his suit was discolored. He looked back at the young man.

"Take you," he said. "You don't want to be following the bloody ballet to St. Petersburg."

But, I saw in the young man's expression that this was precisely his desire. It was all that he wanted—and in the older man's face, I caught the look of a man afraid of losing a vital companion.

"The first time I saw Perrot, he danced like a fisherman. And as soon as I laid eyes on him, when I saw the silence and speed of his movements, I said to myself: that man could break houses. If there had been dust on the stage, he never would have disturbed it."

The young man spoke, finally. "I thank you for your hospitality, for inviting me here, and for the drink, Sir, but you have me quite wrong. I want to go abroad with the Company. I don't think that I have or can offer what it is that you are looking for. The Company—"

Abruptly, the man reached across the table and snatched the young man's unfinished beer from him. I watched as he drained it, the white stubble moving on his throat. "All right, then. You ponce off, back to your theatre. But when you're a third tier nobody, starving in the snow, don't forget that I tried to foist the good life on you."

Straightening his jacket, the young man rose gracefully. As he passed me, squeezing through the drinkers toward the street, I heard him call the man a pig. The seat vacated by the young man was the only gap in the crowded pub. Intrigued and exhausted, I sat down there. Registering me by inclining his head, the man in the red cravat continued to speak and hold forth as if I were merely his latest appointment.

"You look tired, son," he said. "Long journey?"

"It was, yes."

He reached out to shake my hand. "My name is Sickert."

"Kurtz. Edward. I heard you talking with that dancer. Is it true that you're a burglar, then? That's quite a thing to discuss openly, Mr. Sickert. Is that how you make your money?"

"Not me, boy. I'm an artist."

He looked at his fingers, flexing them.

Just then, a woman, surely a prostitute, passed close to our table through the tangled crowd. As she made her way by, she leered toward the old man, straightening his wool cap with dirty fingers, her eyes lowered lasciviously. "Evenin', Julian."

"Later, love. Not now. Get lost, eh?" Almost as she had gone, he reached out and groped at her buttocks. He held up his hand, showing me his palm. "Brick dust," he explained in a laconic tone. "Annie's been a busy girl." I saw that the girl had deliberately disturbed his pretensions, and that this was his means of striking back at her, in a mild way. He grinned at me before taking a good draught of his beer. "Shall we have another?" He put his fingers to his lips and made a piercing whistle.

"I'm looking for work," I explained, as a girl brought two more beers.

"Work? That's a laugh. How old are you?"

"Sixteen, Sir." I lied, adding a year. "Do you know of anything?"

"Maybe. But who needs employment?"

Sickert was not his real name. His real name, such as any of us possesses one, was Mallard or Maybrick. I would come to hear these names employed most interchangeably. I heard these from the landlord of The George, from a Constable on his patrol, and from a lamplighter as we made our way through the wet doldrums of the city, drifting through the benighted Elephant and Castle. Furtively, he explained his trades. A banker hastening through the fog greeted him as Maybrick. Another prostitute, an exhausted silhouette in the sunrise, insinuated: "A little of what you fancy, Mr. Maybe?" A butcher, loading carcasses, called out from his dingy shop front, "'Ello Mallard!" So many assumed to know him, and yet no one knew him at all. I flatter myself to suggest that I knew him best. It is perhaps the truth. Immediately, as I recollect these matters, I recognize that my transit from Charleville was manipulated at a subterranean level by men who worked on me with the hard and brilliant chisels of their personalities, and who were yet soluble as ghosts: my father, Eric Paine, Julian Maybrick, men whose very potency was a fact of their ultimate invisibility.

Brutality and disappearance are the twin reliefs of my existence. They are opposite coin faces where one visage justifies the other: my father, and myself, tossed hither and thither—brutality and disappearance. Let me tell you, when one truly feels a sense of one's own guilt to be innate, inalienable, tumorous, then one must invent and seek out reasons for it. Even now, writing to you from this jungle with its emerald, scarlet and bell-black, with its muddy water and bloody ivory, I feel like an accused innocent in search of his crime. My heart is broken. It is my fault that she died. It is my fault that he abandoned us. Every time that I ran away from that house in Charleville as a boy, he beat her black and blue. He jabbed mutation into her with his brute knuckles. In dismay, my guilt goes out from me, distressing the world, imploring its attention with weird violence. Disappearance is also an act of violence. Do not imagine that my erasure is not an intentional cruelty. Yet, it is also bought at a price of pain, to be always a mote in a faraway sunset, immolated in the fierce heat of nothingness—*Au-delà l'au-delà*—beyond the beyond.

One night, heavy with alcohol, wandering the city, we passed through Mitre Square and Maybrick took me to his lodgings. The stairs echoed underfoot as we climbed his sinister tenement. He had promised that he would show me his work, and that there might be a role in it for me. As we entered, framed in the smoky evanescence of the moon, he staggered to his single dirty window, and flung it wide open. The room reeked from a stagnant chamber pot, and something like carrion. He lit two lamps, apologizing for the condition of his berth, and explained that he had, while intoxicated, dropped a piece of kidney upon the floor more than a week ago, but he had not been able to find it. "Like when you know you've dropped a coin, but you never heard it hit the ground," he said. This was not surprising. It was a cramped garret furnished with a narrow bed covered with a gray wool blanket, and a simple table. But the table, the bare floorboards, and half of the bed were littered with newspaper clippings, writing paper, all torn and crushed, some of it stained or scorched, as though the room had been ransacked. I watched as Maybrick strode toward the corner of the room, to the right of the open window, cursing under his breath. Crouching in a dune of paper, he retrieved the end of a length of twine that I now saw should have been strung across the place like a clothesline. Maybrick wound the line back onto the doglegged six-inch nail, from which it had come undone. The rest of the line rose up from within the detritus on the floor. Papers dangled from the string by clothespins, reminiscent of pennants in a ship's rigging. Then I was amazed, and Maybrick saw this, for he announced:

"My finest work! Fortunately, they must have dried before the line slipped the nail." The papers that hung on this thread were money, £5 notes. Suddenly, I saw the meaning of all of the scattered leaves about me.

"You're a forger," I said.

"Kurtz," he said, shaking his head, "I am *the* forger." He handed me one of the monochrome bank notes. "Course, it's so much harder now that they're *printing* the bastards. What do you think?"

"Honestly, I don't know. I've never seen or held a real one. Do they work?"

"I don't know. But, we'll find out soon enough. You're going to try one out."

I began to protest.

"But, it'll have to wait a day, because tomorrow's Sunday. The banks'll be closed and I have to go to church."

"Church? You, Julian?"

"I play the organ," he said. "I used to play piano at a dance school, but there's no longer any place for me there. A girl accused me of something horrible. So, I bang out a few hymns and siphon off the collection money. But, that's got to come to an end." The forger said: "You demonstrate these fivers for me, and I—" He busied his hands among the papers on the table before holding up a document to the lamplight. "I'll give you one of these." He handed it to me before getting down on his knees and fumbling beneath his bed for a pair of beer bottles.

The document had an unfinished look to it. "What is it?"

"An Oxford education."

*Crocodiles in sepia—rain on brown surf—*I got back to Jamaica Road after midnight. Mrs. Albert was beside herself. I saw her from a distance, standing outside the tenement, leaning against the coal-streaked door. She held a lamp in her hand, surveying the cold street. She was wearing a black shawl about her shoulders, shaking with exhausted echoes of what had surely been sobs a few minutes ago. Now she saw me, and she raised her other hand, drawing it across her tears. When I got close enough, and could hear the fear in her breath, I saw that in wiping away her tears, she had drawn a blindfold of soot across her eyes. "I'm sorry, Ma," I said.

"I thought you was gone, Edward."

"I brought you something."

We went inside and climbed the stairs to what passed for her kitchen. From my pocket, I withdrew one of Maybrick's notes that I had taken from his drying line while he had been retrieving the beer. I told her, "This is the first."

On Sunday morning, I went to the church where Maybrick claimed to be the organist, and I took Ma Albert, suggesting that we should be thankful for the fortune that providence had bestowed. There he was—*sans cravat*—and without his cap, his gray hair streaming over his gabardine collar. His back was to us, shoulders undulating as he played underneath the tall golden pipes, a mad god ejected from the pantheon of civilized thought and laws, still hanging on at the rim of life. For all of his cynicism, he was a nostalgic creature, after all—*Then fancies fly away, He'll not fear what men say; He'll labor night and day to be a pilgrim*—

There was a red sun over Waterloo Bridge the next day as we walked the Thames Embankment. Maybrick fished a flask of grog from the pocket of his coat, distractedly eyeing the long boats at the opposite bank. "Sanger's barges," he said. "More exotic creatures for his cages and tents." The tide was iron gray and just as slow. He handed me the flask. Sipping at it brought me a strange dewy clarity. We had barely slept, having let the drink and the promise of the counterfeit money keep us awake. Maybrick had told me that his treasure would allow him to penetrate deeper into the fathoms of the city. I think that I must have passed out for a short while, sitting on the floor of his garret, with my back against the wall. Whatever he saw across the river, I could not, and we walked on.

The morning boats began their coffin-like shunting, and I thought of my mother, my lost dog sleeping beside her, floating on the Channel. The fishbone feel of grief stuck in my throat. I have never learned to be cavalier with it. I wanted to be a boy again, running toward the Belgian border. The pain was overwhelming. Within the lapse of a single week, I had lost everything. I thought of Mrs. Albert, and wondered where her ancestors were . . . Paris, Berlin, Catalonia, Budapest? I would make things right for her. I understood that the journey was, is, and will always be irrational.

"Heron."

Maybrick pointed at the mudflats. I believe that he was nervous. I asked him where we would test the forged money. He wanted it to pass the sternest examination first, so we wove into the city until he found the bank he wanted. "This is your moment, Edward. Take one of these inside." Before trusting me with it, he crushed the note in his fist, and then pressed it flat, wrapping it against the stem of a lamppost. "I opened an account a week ago with a bit of real money. Go inside. Tell the bankers you work for Mr. Jacks and that this is his deposit. If you can bank it, I'll give you another for yourself. If they rumble you, well, I suppose these won't be any good for your bail. So, this might be goodbye, cousin."

"I'll see you in a minute, Maybrick. Don't worry."

Fraud provided what breeding could not. I strode from the cold mausoleum of that bank with the confidence of a young demon, the echoes of my heels ringing behind me through the vault. Maybrick was leaning against his lamppost, and as he saw me, his grin spread like a frying white yoke. His hands were in his pockets, and his great coat shrugged on his back as he shook his hidden fists in euphoria. A foxy *yes* hissed across the street as I approached him. His accent sunk into river-deep Cockney: "You done it, Kurtz. You only bloody done it!" He clapped his hand upon my shoulder.

"I only paid the fiver in. You made the money, Maybrick."

"Stone me, I'm better than I thought." Unbuttoning his coat, and folding it over his shoulder, he murmured through his teeth, projecting to me like an actor, "I'm a rich man, Kurtz."

"What will you do?"

"Nothing—nothing for now, at least. I'll finish up some business, send a few postcards, and then slip away, well away, with as little ostentation as possible."

"You'll go abroad? I thought you wanted to stick it out in London first, to rub peoples' noses in it."

"O, I will, but the whole world is on the move. There are no real countries anymore. Let people believe there are, but it is merely paper—so much *paper*." At this, he took one of his false notes, ripped it in pieces, and pushed the shreds into his mouth, the ink staining his lips. "Like your education. I haven't forgotten. Come on. Let's go to The George."

I spent one more night, cloaked in a venous fur on Maybrick's floor. In some unlit hour, I don't know what time it was, I found him awake, writing by candlelight at his table, his one gray blanket wrapped about his shoulders. His face turned slightly in the flame, but he made no effort to conceal his work. A stench hung over him, and flies whined in tight arcs over the tweezers he held in his left hand.

"What on earth are you doing?" I whispered.

"I'm writing to the police."

"What? But—"

"Not about *you*. No, I just . . . I just I found that bit of kidney." With inexplicable tenderness, he slipped the organ inside one of his envelopes—or rather it was a narrow cardboard box, like the larger type of matchbox. "Will you send this for me, in the morning? It's the last thing I'll ask of you. Someone will be looking for it."

"I don't understand."

"Don't try."

That smell. I had denied it on the beach at Calais, when it slithered through the cracks in my mother's casket, salted by the breath of the English Channel. Now it came back to me in the gleaming lanes of London, on streets like sullied glass. My mother came through the fog. I saw her in Buck's Row, a bonnet dangling from one ear like seaweed, toothless in the wet lamplight, a red wash spilling from her distended abdomen. From Hanbury Street, she stuck out her tongue at me, bearing her intestines across her shoulder like a pet octopus, swiveling in a mist of bad blood, projecting the oxidized hollows of her cervix. I saw her again, dressed in black, bleeding in Dutfield's Yard— her white hand was extended toward me, holding a lozenge for her breath, her red throat gaping. Back in Mitre Square, she came again, her tart coat parted, her stomach swinging open like vaudeville curtains, a great wave of gore pouring across the cobbles toward my feet, the tripe on her shoulders soft and steaming. The last time I saw her was Miller's Court, where the hemorrhage was complete, and in that horror where consciousness knows to submerge a thought forever, I understood that I would never see her again.

They must have taken her off on the Calais side. I found no mention of any lost body floating on the sea in *The Daily Telegraph,* or anywhere else. Her testament would not be honored, not bodily. Although something of her drifted and continued over the bloody cobblestones and whispered down Fleet Street and to Great Scotland Yard. Just before dawn, I let Maybrick's small package fall into a red postbox, and, pushing my hands into my coat pockets, I felt more of the counterfeit money that I had taken from him. I could not return to his company. In delirium, I slept rough beneath railway arches. I suppose that I could have taken a very fine room in a very fine hotel with those notes, but the shocks from witnessing those aspects of my ancestry in the terrible streets left me desirous of little but punishment, and by the same token, an anaesthetizing freeze in the veins. As the trains shook the red bricks behind my skull, I thought how cruel blood is. I awoke lost. I think that Maybrick left for Liverpool and a ship the following day. He seemed so spectrally connected to London that I overheard conversations concerning him more than once in the months that came after. As I write, that was a little more than four years ago.

Cenotaph of tusks—kerosene on the lagoon—violet scent of palm oil—Nsumbu is quite angry with me this morning. He asks me why I "make risk" and to be conscientious in my account, his demand leaves me paralyzed, for I cannot explain why. When I swallow, dumb, my Adam's apple swings low and heavy as a barge sack in my throat. For as much as we both know better: the jungle cannot kill me, nor the brown river drown me—he has become attached to me after a strange paternal fashion. Entering my hut this morning, he looked at me with the furious relief of a child who was afraid that his father might not be home for Christmas. I had been walking, I explained. A dream had woken me. To perambulate as men once did, antediluvian, thuggish, hunched in the upright chaos of the night forest is one of the more sublime experiences left to a man. Even in daylight, with the sun high over the tree masts, a saturated gloom prevails, but then it might be split with irruptions of vivid color as a man is taken by a leopard—freckled gold and a bright plume of blood. I wonder, is this not like any city on the globe? Save that here, in the intransigent Congo, one is not compelled by roads nor pavement, or civilizing lines. Certainly, there are some tracks and trails, but more generally, one meanders in fruitless ellipses that nevertheless draw freedom in its most absolute.

Her long legs come poling through the tall grass, glistening in the rain. Above the level of the grass, this swaying power, this ancient shadow of love, this nigger Magdalene. The sunlight catches on the ebony knots of her collarbone as she drifts, serene, lethal and luminous.

Nsumbu, he is the only man I have permitted to know the location of The Pit. The Pit was excavated a month after I came to this deep station. A dozen men, tall, slender, like turned licorice, flowed through the jungle. Nsumbu helped with the blindfolds. We led the blind men, all threaded on one long rope, each of them carrying a pick or a shovel—some pairs of men carried wooden ladders between them. Others brought woven sections that resembled hunting breaks, thatched partition walls. By the time we stopped our procession, none of them could have told where they were, and as night bore down, even the vague shadows of the canopy that might have been discerned through their blinkers in the bloody sunset dissolved into the greater darkness of the nocturnal country. In a circle, they hacked at the earth. For hours, I watched them digging. The moonlit nubs of their heads bowed and vanished into the soil. They went down in silence, nervous of Nsumbu's whip. A dank fog of sweat and hard breath rose out of the earth as they mined. When the sun rose again, I was pleased with the cavity. Nsumbu called the slick men to climb the ladders out. Their blindfolds were soaked and dirty, and as they grimaced in exhaustion I could see soil even between their teeth, as though they had resorted to eating their way into the mud when their arms failed them. Behind them they left a crater, a bowl, the lightless grail into which I could pour my life. The thatched walls went around it, and the blindfolded men roofed it over with Nsumbu as their eyes. From a few feet back into the jungle, it was almost indistinguishable from the derelict forest.

Milk-faced pilgrims rot in sanguinary grass—Bibles leaves— gaping at the water—With Maybrick gone to god knows where, the forgery of my education slowly mutated like a shadow down a pale wall, becoming an obscure insult to me. I carried it in my pocket. It pulsed and cajoled me. It would not fit me, not my age, nor proletarian accent. It is hard to impersonate oneself, to carry off what one would like to be without the first clue of how that man might live, what he might say. In a manner, I became mute. Certainly, the counterfeit money could swathe my past with a kind of glamor, but the forging of my mind, I could not, somehow, stand. Part of me was still floating a paper boat in a puddle, staring dumbly at a parading butcher, dreaming in the slow shadow of a French watermill. While the money lasted, I would have no need of work. I could spend my time bettering myself. And so I took to trawling the British Library, the museums and galleries, and even the graveyards to look upon great men, and then back to read about them, to memorize headstone verses, to make my marrow fit its bones, to force my intellect and cant to meet their credentials. All the poetry of the churchyard pointed to the green future from the green past—*No, no, go not to Lethe, neither twist Wolf's-bane, tight-rooted, for its poisonous wine*—I was happy. Now, I am far into the reach of oblivion. My station marks the sweet still of death, the lagoon of endless luxury. I am happier, yet. My mistake, in those days when I found myself lost in the sudden chaos of my mother's death, my betrayal of her, my seduction, was to believe that I might find myself in that city of destruction.

Dawn, red and white—My Intended, I am thinking now of when we met. It was during my last year in London. Shivering even in my mohair coat, I was standing beside the grave of Karl Marx, in Highgate Cemetery, the last leaves of counterfeit bank notes crushed into my pocket, the hydra of opium imposing on my veins. The molecular grass rippled and whispered and a brilliant ladybird tracked across the stone. The grave was infringed with ivy and desiccated flowers. Most men are faithful to their pasts, to the good gore of their ancestry. If I were such a man, I would be derelict in some ghetto of Poland or London or Prague, churning in a freezing gutter of guilt. The eastern quadrant of the cemetery was empty in the morning, save for the stirring of the vines and way the untended slab hummed with the unintelligible emptiness of a life's work. I knew that death is small: a mosquito bite, the poison of the tsetse fly, or the first infinitesimal bud of a tumor—*All that is solid melts into air, all that is holy is profaned, and man is at last compelled to face with sober senses his real conditions of life, and his relations with his kind—*

You came out of the silence, dew coalescing the apparition of a young woman. I was startled, for I had not heard your approach, and shifted furtively away from the grave as if I were ashamed. As you materialized, tightening the fox fur stole about your shoulders, I saw through that russet pelt, glimpses of the expensive pearls at your throat—a throat like ivory, I thought, even then. Inevitably, I must wonder now if there is anything more to it, for me. Is all of this carnage, a mere homage to something I possessed so very merely, that was beyond my station? Was there a moment when I might have been otherwise? I was hungry. You wore a blue dress, and a thin blue vein close to your temple caught my eye as I told you my name, and made to shake hands. You wore grey leather gloves that you peeled from warm fingers, wearing no rings. I told you that I was lost. There was a funeral I had meant to attend, but I had been detained, and I had been looking for the plot. I gave you a nip of brandy, for you appeared exhausted with melancholy, and I asked if I might walk you to the gates. After the iron railings, we continued to walk together, and fell into a coffee house like weary siblings. This chance, this coincidence is the quintessence of genius, longing, and the beginning of anomie. There was a newspaper left on the table where we were seated, and I told the girl I should like to keep it.

"Do you know this actor, Mansfield, the American?" You pointed at an advertisement for the Lyceum Theatre.

"I've heard the rumors . . ."

"Yes!" I remember the way you caught your rising voice like a bird in a fist, suddenly embarrassed by the animation in your face, distracted from mourning. In my selfishness, I had never inquired why you were at the cemetery. I simply took our encounter for granted. The matrices of this jungle prove that there really is no chance. As the girl brought our coffee, and you stirred the sugar in, you continued, almost at a whisper. "Did he really murder those women, do you think? They say that his transformation into that monster on the stage is uncanny." I was preoccupied with a drop of dew from your wrist that had begun to traverse the Mons Venus of your palm. I watched it rill along your ivory hand until it met the silver gleam of the teaspoon. I reached out and closed your fingers in mine, gently taking the spoon from you, before closing my mouth over it. That evening, we investigated the transforming actor for ourselves, grease-paint shining on the man devouring man. I wondered what had become of Maybrick.

Daybreak, silver and tar—In the autumn of the following year, during the London Dock Strike of 1889, I chanced upon one of the men who had skulked away from my past. He drifted in front of me as though we were two mariners thrown by the same sea storm. The night before, I had been gone walking from Tower Bridge toward Limehouse, its secretive opium dens and the Regent's Canal Dock. I had been there before. The number of Chinamen I have encountered, I could count with one hand, but I saw them all in Limehouse. This was prior to my twenty-fourth birthday in October, still some weeks away. Within me was an ember of savage poetry. I wanted to write it out, to expose it to the combustion of a public outing. Perhaps this was what my father felt as he touted his bare knuckles around illegal rings. The place was unmarked. The trick was to loiter close to the shadows until one of the frontages revealed itself with a slight creaking of a door and a strange whisper of broken English.

Through an opening like peeling yellow skin, the Chinaman who I knew as Yang admitted me. He was middle-aged, his skin taut across the harsh angles of his face, a thin moustache growing unevenly over his liverish lip. The Limehouse façade gave way to what seemed like a strange and gaudy rift in the city, reaching back into the walls of the Thames. Satins hung in the sweetened air. Yang played with a loose front tooth, manipulating it with his red tongue in the weak lantern light of the doorway. Readily, I made my way in.

Yang manhandled me, directing me closer to one of his paper lanterns, to better study my clothes, making little clicks with his tongue. With my surfeit of money, I had adopted narrow tailored trousers, a black brocaded waist-coat, and a topcoat of lead-gray mohair. Yang turned my lapel over, humming approvingly at the fold. He took me by the elbow and we began toward the smoking rooms. Each partition of Yang's den was dubbed after a creature of the Chinese zodiac. The place was not altogether as squalid as you might imagine, and Yang himself was clean, wore cologne and a simple suit. I requested The Dragon Room, as I had for each of my visits during the past six months, working on wounds that will never heal. The Dragon Room was decorated with watercolors of hysterical serpents, rolling their eyes, undulating sensuously in their biting. Yang wiped dust from one of his murals with a silk hand-kerchief. After paying him, I took a long pipe and reposed upon a ripped red divan.

I dreamed that my father had been imprisoned in Poland. I rolled in silver wreaths of bliss.

When I emerged from my *petit orient* into the Limehouse morning, nothing moved, except for the fog passing in white eddies over the barges along the Embankment, and I upon my walk back to the west. Coal waited in wet heaps. Smeared tomcats slept in the bunkers, while cargo chests tilted on the gentle current, nailed shut. The winches and ropes were still. Unlike the dock strikes in Southampton, the resistance in London had been violent. I had read about clashes in the newspaper. The first eerie signal of what was to come was the shape of something tall rising out of the vapor. It swayed nervously, a stalk of ochre-yellow and brown elongating high into the air. At first, I took it to be some hangover of the night before, the return of some old dragon. Then, I saw its eyes and the lick of its prehensile tongue—*a giraffe*. This was my first glimpse of one, materializing unnaturally upon the Embankment, its head appearing to swivel pitifully in confusion. A shipload of exotic animals was being unloaded. Some were being readied to make their way to the zoo along Regent's Canal, and others were being tethered to bollards on the quayside to await some other less careful transport.

Then the first muffled sounds reached me, of the strike-breakers and scabs. Between those human sounds came other animal sounds, some stirring on the jetty, pulling listlessly at the ropes, drugged, exhausted or too cold to struggle. Two men led the giraffe along the dockside toward a large cage, borne on the back of a sizeable carriage to be drawn by horses. Behind this came a skinny elephant calf. Unconsciously, as though I had broken in upon a dream, I moved through the fog, approaching fragmentary glimpses of these creatures, the yells of some primates hanging in the air. The men who led them were hired blacklegs, Sunday morning drunks, and cons.

Someone must have alerted the striking dockers, for as I passed along alongside The Swan Inn, a gang of men emerged from one of the streets that led to the Thames. There were fifty of them, dressed in their navy sack coats and hobnail boots, scarves around their throats; these they removed and stuffed into their pockets. The dockers, seeing the scabs unloading, began a slow clapping, an ironic applause that froze the blacklegs on their spots. Some of the dockers stamped their boots in unison, an ominous warning, with the slapping of their hands. They began to advance slowly along the towpath, and I pushed myself back against the wall of the Inn to let them by. The men leading the giraffe had not yet tethered it on the dockside. Instead, they let go of their ropes, striking it on the flanks with their fists. Afraid of the stones beneath it, the animal did not move, and suffered more beatings as it trembled. Gradually, it began to scuff and skid on the cobblestones as the mob swarmed the barge. I could no longer tell striker from scab in the confusion, though evidently the dockers knew. Two dockers grabbed the reins of the elephant calf and dragged it aside. It raised its trunk, letting out a short blast of fear. As the fight spread and men began to cry out in fury and pain, the giraffe finally reared, its neck contorting, folding back like a great whip. Even above the shouts of the struggle, I heard a sound like a splintering plank. One of the animal's legs snapped as its hooves slipped on the wet stones. It made no other sound as it fell, collapsing in a terrible twist of limbs. Somehow, my eyes fixed upon one of the men who had led it and beaten it. The mob careened along the side of the river, a tidal wave of men filling the road and the towpath. He collided with me. Our heads cracked together. My sickness at the fallen giraffe, a mangled giant dying beneath the riot, and the sudden warp of the Thames in my pain threatened to overthrow me. Yet, I refused to go down. As the torrent of men crashed about us, fighting to keep my footing, I grabbed at the sleeve of his coat. Men cried out: "Scab! Scab!" The scab whose coat I had gripped began to slip on the wet cobblestones. Our eyes met as I hauled him upright, both of us bleeding from cuts on our eye sockets. In bewilderment and shock I saw him grinning at me. I knew his smirk. Pulsing tears wet my face. All this transpired in a matter of a second, and a flash of recognition. It was the one I had known from the beach at Calais. "Eric Paine!" Still grappling after the clash, our faces were as close as mine had been to my mother's as I struggled with her body in its casket across the wet beach to the steamer, eight years before. An ache, such as a sound lost in fog that grows louder as it clears, pulsed within me. Before I could identify it, it became an agony. He had convinced me to abandon my mother's corpse on that steamer, and now my betrayal of her stood bleeding, grimacing with confusion before me. I fancied that he knew me. I hooked my leg behind his knee and shoved him down. In an instant I was on top of him, his skull between my hands as I smashed him against the dockside. His head began to open and his life began to seep out through the cracks in a hot red yolk. Men grabbed at me, trying to haul me away from him. It was only after his brain had slipped out like a gray terrine that the dockers hauled me away from his inert body. Piercing police whistles broke the mob. The constables took me, caked in blood, to the station. All the while, I shook like a freezing man. Dressed as I was, and with money in my pockets, it was obvious that I was not a striking dockworker. One of the constables insinuated something about Cleveland Street that I did not then understand. I protested that I was a poet on my way back to France. I had become trapped in other men's violence.

"A fucking dandy poof gone mad in Limehouse. Shirt-lifter goes berserk! I can see the bleedin' 'eadlines," the detective at the station said. "You smell funny," he offered, sniffing the opiate smoke lingering in my jacket. "Banging the gong, was it, you French wanker?"

I wept in a uremic cell, but I was lucky. I might have hanged like Monsieur Prudhomme. But none of the dockworkers came forward to identify me as the killer of the scab Lancaster. Someone came forward and suggested that the emaciated elephant calf had trampled him in the middle of the riot, and that I was trying to resuscitate him when the police arrived. The dockers could brook an accident, but a murder would arouse the wrong journalists. There was just enough doubt to keep me from swinging, and I made bail with Maybrick's false fivers—too many of them. I heard that they shot the elephant calf, and the broken legged giraffe was euthanized beside the barges.

I recall the first afternoon at your father's house a few days later, his diplomatic apartments, and his rictus of distaste as I responded to his suspicions. Taking me in my mohair coat to be an insouciant dandy and a dilettante, he wanted to know my ideas for supporting you in the manner to which you were entitled. I told him that I wrote poems, and indeed, I could paint, but these were trifles, he was correct. Trying not to breathe gin into the room, my conscience curled in on itself like a Charleville grub beneath his polished shoe. Under the rain of my station, I wonder now if he is still alive. Would I not have heard if he had died? He appeared to me ripe for a coronary. I had been drinking in Hyde Park, watching a greyhound being walked, before forcing myself along Upper Grosvenor Street and ringing the bell outside his anthracite door, waiting for one of the servants to answer. There were grass stains on my knees, and I realized as I approached him that one of my shoelaces was untied. One gets used to things about oneself that make others recoil. Still, all autodidacts suffer from a kind of insecurity, the fear of being found out, I am certain. You were standing by one of the three huge windows, and I wondered if you had been able to see me out there on the grass. You were wearing a calico dress and holding a small oriental fan; that I recall well. Lying out there in the grass, I had thought about handing your father my counterfeit Oxford degree. I had it in my pocket that afternoon. From the ignominious moment of my arrival, he regarded me with suspicion and contempt. I thought, yes, this is why I would call myself an anarchist criminal, a communist worker, or a revolutionary beggar. Yet, we held our manner even through our mutual revulsion. I imagined myself protesting with my forged paperwork, stuffing it into your father's cruel, wet mouth as he went on. How, again, did I propose to keep you? What work was I engaged in? Where did my family come from? I recall the glances between you, the barely perceptible flush in your white complexion telling of a deep trench of anger. For an instant, your father with his silver muttonchops and mine with his broken nose were one man. That man turned his back on me on the tidal mud of Calais, and I felt myself caught in the slow sneer of the other's paternity, about to be cast out of that smoky study, with breeding, fists, and ancient currencies set against me. I think that your father had observed the way my cut-glass accent shifted when one of his servants announced the tea service. I confess that it did not offend me that you might be employing me as a means of spiting your father, but even you had no measure of the fathoms of my abjection. I suppose that I struggle to justify involving you. Perhaps it was out of some cowardly instinct to have some ties to society, even as I secretly planned to abandon it. I let out the bait.

"There is a company, sir, that has business in Africa," you observed helplessly as your father lunged.

"Yes, indeed, how edifying!" My hook protruded from his aristocratic jowl. "And, would you believe, I know a man?"

"I have no letter of recommendation, unfortunately."

Your old man was experiencing an epiphany. He could get me out of the country, altogether. Furthermore, I would almost certainly die on some benighted delta with a spear waving from my dysentery-swollen abdomen. He no longer cared that I might I use the two of you for decent meals and cab fares, to buy the auspices of an officer. Anything less would be *most retrograde to our desire.*

But, even as your father and I made our pact, a shade of me rising from a damask settee to press my white thumbs into his throat, I think I may have sobbed gently in my hammock as the red sun rose. I experienced myself awakening to this melancholy station, and the gravity of my immense property holding me, the everyday violence of being God. It was the memory of all this, carried in dream, that woke me, and set me walking before dawn again, back to The Pit, and why Nsumbu is sulking with his rifle, outside in my *cordon sanitaire* of shrunken skulls.

*Sap—mosquitoes—my palace in the black mangroves—*The Pit is the End of Guilt. The Pit, like an inverted pleasure dome is filled with my ivory. There, I repose upon a subterranean throne of tusks. The wings of my ivory throne are adorned with the viridescent eyes of long Congo peacock feathers. Golden leopard skins and broad zebra hides line the floor. Parrot flowers grow in champagne bottles that I shift under the sloping needles of sun that penetrate the thatched ceiling—a Venus flytrap in a shaving dish. Hundreds of tusks rise like stalagmites in the pinhole light. Elephant guns, ammunition and ration cases are stacked against the gentle parabola of the interior—quinine, tins of Lambert and Butler's navy cut tobacco, the corroding image of Queen Victoria painted on a tin of biscuits, soldered shut, Crosse and Blackwell's anchovy paste, jars of Nsumbu's palm wine, bottles of claret, champagne, whisky, cigarettes, madras, matches, oil, and tins of sardines. A spare uniform, unworn, hangs from a buffalo horn. It is beyond me to imagine ever putting it on. My gorgeous white sentinels curl about me. Here is my cool solitude, everything that I will not give to the Company, the treasure that I keep for myself. The Pit is a moment elongating in all the directions of Eternity. Crawling through the slim fissure in the ground, the nightmares roll back, stripped like old skin. The half-caste has gone back to the Company with enough to satisfy them.

I am almost alone. Down here, in my rich black basin, I can leave even myself. What is Kurtz?

My Intended,

The crones were knitting in the waiting room, as if the pair of them had been peeled from a pack of nicotine-stained tarot cards, a massive skein of ebony wool spooling about them like a puddle of hot tar. It ran across the marble floor at me, filling the Company offices with a gothic flag. They wore identical smoke colored dresses, imitating the Royal British fashion in widowing. The more emaciated of the two, her complexion drawing tight to her bones, reminded me of Yang the opium master, except that I liked Yang instantly. She put her needles down, glancing viciously at the sun streaming through the tall windows. She muttered something in old Flemish. At this, the other witch rose to her feet, pushing the huge black fleece from her knees. This one, apparently younger and healthier, yet still bent beneath her fats with arthritis, traversed the waiting room in the manner of a leaden chess piece. She lowered the venetian blinds with sullen irritation. Painfully, she returned to her little rococo chair. It was the shade of powdered pink with fuchsia upholstery embroidered with white tulips. The two witches struck me as hysterical. I must have been laughing for some moments before I became aware of the sound of my amusement echoing back from the hard white walls. The elder crone hissed at me.

"Casse-toi."

"Let it come down," I said.

A secretary emerged from an anteroom to my right. She introduced herself as Madame De Clercq. She was a lithe woman, gliding efficiently and brightly about the vast building. Her graying blonde hair was worn in a tight bun. She beckoned me into her office. It resembled a small library with index cards in mahogany drawers. There was another door at the back of the room. She seated herself behind her L-shaped desk and riffled through some papers. I recognized my handwriting on some of them. On the right-angled wing of her desk was a gleaming Remington typewriter. She saw me eyeing it. "Mr. Stanley brought it," she said.

"Who are the old bags?" I asked.

"Leopold's aunts." Her voice was quick and flat. "You'll see the Doctor presently. You're French?"

"A piece of me."

"Well, the British have their blood up this year. I expect to see more of them coming through, journeymen, opportunists. How is your hygiene, Mr. Kurtz?"

I held out my hands, turning them over for her.

"Biting your fingernails to the quick does not necessarily make you cleaner," she said. A bell sounded from above the other door. "Doctor Severijns will see you now." She turned toward her typewriter and began writing me up.

Severijns was a small, disheveled man, and his tobacco beard was streaked with silver. I recall that his head thrust through the doorframe before I could cross the room to his surgery. He rang the brass bell again, feigning a cough as though he were possessed by a frantic haste to process me. The secretary ignored him, continuing to type at her Remington. Severijns clasped my hands, intoning in a low, earnest voice, "Welcome, welcome." The blinds of his surgery were closed. An eclectic collection of lamps illuminated his furniture. His red divan was furred with dust. Above the fireplace was a portrait of the King. Indeed, I realized that there was such a painting hanging in every room of the Company offices, his Abrahamic beard cascading over his blue uniform, pristine golden epaulettes shimmering in the oily light. Without loyalty to him, I had failed to register his presence. Upon Severijn's mantelpiece, flanked by a bleached cadre of cracked primate skulls, was a framed photograph of a mustachioed man wearing a perforated helmet and an ornately braided white uniform.

"Mr. Stanley, I presume."

The Doctor boasted: "Inscribed to me, no less, on the reverse, with kind words. Quite the famous gentleman, our Mr. Stanley."

I said nothing.

Severijns yanked a stethoscope from the pocket of his gabardine coat. "Will you undress, please?" I had barely unbuttoned my shirt before he advanced upon me, pressing the cold device against my chest. The earpieces hung in a disordered manner about his large ears. After barely a second, without listening to my heart, he declared: "Fit enough, quite fit enough for there." He discarded the hoses. "It's significantly less a question of *physical* fitness, anyhow. You can dress again. Remember to take your arsenic tablets, use a charcoal filter, even for the rainwater. That mousy *Barnet* of yours—that's the correct word, yes?"

"Barnet Fair: hair. Yes."

"Ha, I heard the Britisher in you. It won't survive. Your hair, that is."

"I know. I've seen how."

"It'll turn white. Good to cut it off," Severijns advised, "and remain in the shade."

"I'm not a vain creature," I said.

"Non—?"

"You want me to look like one of those." I pointed to one of the porcelain heads on his shelves, functioning as bookends. They were mapped over, like globes.

"I'm a phrenologist, foremost, Mr. Kurtz. I am going to measure your cranium. Any syphilis, lunacy among your ancestors?"

I shook my head.

"When you come back to us, I'll measure you again. Proximity, miscegenation, atmospheres—all of it may alter the structure of your skull."

"Astonishing! Will I feel the . . . these alterations?"

"Is anything felt in the transit between pupa and imago? I think not."

"But you're insinuating a reverse development, from butterfly to grub."

Severijns put his finger to his lips. "And you said you weren't vain," he said. "The savages seem to like it well enough. Perhaps it feels better to feel less." The fierce quality returned to his eyes. Between the wart-faced witches and the phrenologist, the secretary was the one merciful conduit. When Severijns was finished with his calipers, working over my skull like a metal spider, I left and encountered the hags again. As if to compound the absurdity, a black cat shrugged against their skeletal ankles. Elated, I walked out into the street.

I took coffee under the arches and arcades of the Grote Markt, the baroque square, spires needling into the overcast skies. Buildings that suggested trellises of coral or carved bones threaded with doves defined the scene. There was a shop selling porcelain tea sets, where of course I bought the set that I have the remnant of with me now. The gold and glass of the guildhalls seemed to breathe in waves when the sun broke the clouds, and the painted facades heaved into animation. I thought of the years it had taken me to reach this place. I contemplated its ages as a besieged city rising from marshes, the operatic burnings, and the factory barricades. I imagined the old river Senne, now bricked under the city, the water paved with new boulevards and industry. Inevitably, as I watched the merchants on the Grand Place,

I thought of Monsieur Prudhomme. What revolutionary fevers fell through the trapdoor of his death? And here, outside the Maison du Roi, now that the King was extending his gloved hand across the globe, yellowing the maps with his imperial acquisitions, how long could he—or any of us—hold off the twilight? There, I remained all day, until night bloomed behind the filigreed buildings. I understood that I had been running toward them, toward my Station, since I was a boy, like a stray dog in search of water.

Je reviendrai, avec des membres de fer, la peau sombre, l'oeil furieux: sur mon masque, on me jugera d'une race forte. J'aurai de l'or: je serai oisif et brutal. Les femmes soignent ces féroces infirmes retour des pays chauds. Je serai mêlé aux affaires politiques. Sauvé. Maintenant je suis maudit, j'ai horreur de la patrie. Le meilleur, c'est un sommeil bien ivre, sur la grève.

It was the end of August 1889, when I stood on Southsea front, having made my pact with the Company. I had taken the train from London to Portsmouth and I was dressed in the navy blue uniform that Nsumbu now wears as he struts about my ivory-choked station. The wind whipped over the Solent, black-headed gulls undulating in the chop. The spray came off the water as though the sea were a great beast shaking its coat dry. I had not told you that I had joined up, let alone that I was leaving. All of this preceded you in my intentions. Standing on the esplanade, I might have been standing upon the edge of a cliff, the white rampart of a widow's empire. The chalk cliffs extended east toward Brighton and Dover, and west beyond Portsmouth toward Land's End, eroded infinitesimally by the dazzling sea. Out to sea, the cylindrical forts of Spitbank, Horse Sand, and No Man's Land stood sentinel, their guns surveying the straight. Perhaps Victoria in her blacks and contracted grief could see it. Yet, what did she want? Some of the people sensed it too, no doubt, as I did. Fractions of England were anxious. Her reclusion was a national symptom. In another fifty years it might all be finished, and the majestic white cliffs would be merely the tideline and the limit. With all that, the sea spray and the beautiful sunlight on the gray-green sea, I was happy, and a little proud also. The country where my mother was born would be belligerent and determined for a while longer, and it was fit for me to leave it that way. If her coffin was taken off back on the Calais side, or whether she oscillated uselessly between there and Dover forever, it did not matter. The globe was a ball of colored wax running in the heat of the sun. What belonged to one today, would not tomorrow, or in a hundred years. It seemed foolish to be enthralled by great empires, to vomit beer in a gutter simply because a monarch is up or down, for the miniscule citizens to align their content and the woes with them. Waiting impatiently in my blue uniform, I knew that its struggles of Victoria and of Leopold were not my own and that I should cast off my colonial disguise at the earliest opportunity. All that I required was a simple plot for the experiment of myself.

I took the railway from Portsmouth to Southampton and watched the long estuary from the docks to the open water while I awaited the steamer, the *SS Mandingo II,* that would take me to from there to Matadi. When the ship arrived, I was riddled with knots of anticipation. When we had loaded and were underway, some hours later, all that I could do was to stand close to the bow, gripping the handrail, staring straight ahead. The salt stung my eyes, and the wind over the tide grew bitterly cold, yet there was a profound relief in me. The lanes were crowded with colorful yachts racing from

Cowes, ferries and fishing vessels where new terraces and pavilions flashed in the light. With her twin masts and broad funnel, our steamer cut impressively through the smaller vessels, whose passengers waved toward the people on our deck. Horns blasted and claxons rang. I did not wave, but kept my grip on the iron railing. I watched the haze over the muddy beaches enveloping the gulls and cormorants. The sea traffic thinned and the sounds of our departure faded under the humdrum of the waters. Soon enough, travelling westward out of the Solent, an idiosyncrasy of the Captain, we rounded the Needles lighthouse, the sharp point of the Isle of Wight, that small shrapnel of England in the sea before the Channel. The chalk rock formation, brilliant white and tall, resembled the jawbone and teeth of a vast creature, one last prehistoric grin. One of the passengers, a prospector bound for Durban, complained about the route, passing close to a reef and shallower water than we would have met on the eastern side of the island. In my opinion, it set us in the right mood for the rest of our journey, some racing in the blood. The rigging whistled overhead as I pulled my jacket tighter about me.

Beyond the Breton cape, relatively calm waters in the Bay of Biscay permitted gin and tonics to be served on the *Mandingo*'s deck. Blue porpoises kept pace with the vessel, undulating sweetly though the surface of the Cantabrian waves. Our funnel cloud unfurled behind us and the engines pumped their giant metal heart. At times, the land could not be seen, and then some vague sliver of the French coast would emerge. When the land was invisible, the unbroken seascape gave me a pleasant sensation of falling, as gulls must feel, tilting on their aerial currents. The other passengers were soldiers and speculators, in the main. The ship's steward was equally attentive and courteous to all as he came swaying around the promenade deck with his talismanic silver tray of cocktails. He was a handsome gentleman of about forty years old, in squeaking rubber plimsolls and a white jacket arrayed with medal ribbons. I overheard him describing the ways in which the Zulu Wars had turned his temples gray. Approaching and noting my uniform, he paused before adding an extra measure of gin to my glass. "Good man," he said. "I have to admit that I admire you chaps, working up those bloody waterways. Are you following Captain Fresleven?" I couldn't say that I had heard of him, I admitted, feeling somehow irreverent. The steward opined: "Decent bugger that Fresleven, for a Dane. Would you think it ill-mannered if I were to speak some unsolicited advice, Sir?" I told him that he should continue. "Of the men going down with blue jack, or whatever other illnesses the jungle is soaked with, the common denominator is that these men slow up. They use too much slack time in lying about because of the heat. One should sweat through the humidity, work hard, don't let the poisons remain in your body. Sweat it out." I told him that I intended a furious pace, and he seemed pleased. "That will keep you clean. Best of luck, Sir," he said. Then he continued his rounds, trailing a faint scent of pomade. I sipped at my gin and tonic and watched a sea smoke slowly obscuring a distant part of the Bay. In general, among the passengers aboard the steamer, there was a general optimism, a confidence in machinery, drills, Remingtons and iron pills, charcoal biscuits and industry, and a view of the horizon that was always rosy. The steward, even through his warnings, maintained this positive disposition. Every modern man with his sparkling apéritif considered himself an exception to the rules of Nature. I wondered about this great Dane, Fresleven.

Chevron banks—hippos immolated—wood-fire—We put in at Gibraltar, the Herculean rock pillar at the northern edge of the strait that delimits the Mediterranean and the Atlantic waters. There was time here for *Pernod* and oysters under the westward side of the mountain. The Steward, whose name I learned was Richardson, purchased olives and oils and seemed greatly pleased to commerce with the old Castilian who had set out his stall in one of the limestone streets. As we approached it, I recall that, from the distance of our steamer, the mountain has reminded me of something like a sundial blade, partly overgrown with moss. Now, under the precipice, I could appreciate the striking cliffs, colored by the setting sun. An Arab directed naked slaves along the wharf, heavy irons dragging on the ground between them. Monkeys descended from the promontory and ran among them, a perversion prehistoric and strangely appalling to me—these were the macaques that enjoyed the protection of the mountain. These restive creatures were better nourished than the broken black men. Each of the Negroes wore a noose about his throat that connected him to the slave before him and after him. Their shoulders were raw from whipping, and the reddening peninsula of Gibraltar now swelled blood all around me. The men grimaced, their white teeth large in their sunken faces, eyes barely open to the scene about them. "Yalla, yalla . . ." The Arab pushed the leading man between the shoulders, choking him as he jerked away from the man shackled and roped behind him. There were nine of them, all painfully adjusting their steps. They filed past us, a carrion stink of decay emanating from the line. The clouds shifted from orange to crimson. Richardson stared after them, olive oil dripping from his chin and staining his white jacket. "Honestly," he said, "this is my first time seeing niggers since Hlobane and Kambula." There were tears in the Steward's eyes, and he swallowed fiercely and repeatedly. Time slowed. A soft breeze blew over the wharf. "I don't suppose you've ever fired a Gatling gun, Kurtz," he said. He pushed another olive between his lips with great difficulty. His hands were shaking. A thin whine escaped his throat, before he sniffed in his mucous and growled, shaking his shoulders until the tremors left him. "The final charge is always the worst, the one you can't forget. I wanted to live, damn it, but if you have ever to fire .30 calibers through calf skin shields like paper and into a wall of exhausted screaming men who understand, who *know* deep in the pits of their souls, that you've finally got them beaten, you'll know what the Devil feels like in his finest moments of cruelty—fifty skulls exploding right in front of you, blood and brains washing over the veldt . . ." Slowly, Richardson began to lift his elbow. I understood that he was beginning to raise his hand to salute the chain of slaves. I put my hand on his arm:

"Let's go." We returned to the *Mandingo* where we drank gin on deck as the first stars came out over the harbor. Richardson was embarrassed and dejected.

"I didn't know that was coming," he said.

"Of course you didn't."

"It's a good thing that it's all over for me that way." He glanced down at the medal ribbons over his heart. "This is my first time out of England since . . . This is my first ship. Picked a bloody fine time to come out of a fugue, didn't I, Kurtz?"

"In my experience—to forget, you must remember."

I was less than ten miles from Morocco and the minatory continent of Africa, eleven million miles of heat. I felt that I could reach out my hand and touch it. The mirage-like crests of Mons Abyla, the second pillar, shimmered to the south. In fact, the proximity of the African land mass instilled in me a sudden kind of becalming, a silence in the skull. I was soothed by a strange sense of returning. I had been there before, far down in my vertebrae. The place presented no danger. I was part of a great magnetism. Yet, for now, our iron ship ran along the shoulders of the continent like a tiny bead of sweat on a huge animal. We steamed beyond the pallid minarets of Tangier and the swaying palms over the white port of Casablanca. In the morning, to our port side, the Sahara moved in unimaginable waves of sand, boiling currents rippling out of the glassy dunes. The sun burned our skin, and we were thankful to be aboard a well-appointed ship with calamine lotion and white vinegar to treat the blistering, and champagne to drink, rather than on the land, dying of thirst and exposure. Eventually, we turned to starboard, toward the ancient fragments that made the Canary Islands, where we would put in at Santa Cruz, on the northeastern side of Tenerife.

The Captain of the *Mandingo* was a tall swarthy Welshman from Swansea named Madoc. I met Captain Madoc as he descended to the deck after we were securely anchored, and the fresh-painted gangplank was out. His countenance was brooding, his jaw set with stubble. His hair was cut very short, almost to his scalp, and his thick brows shifted continually, as though every subtle nuance of his perceptions was manifested on his face. "The weather may be unseasonably bad tonight, I'll tell you now. You see that?" He addressed Richardson, indicating a storm that seemed to me far away across the ocean. It looked like a rod of lightless air. I introduced myself to Madoc. Despite his meteorological predictions for us, he was otherwise genial. We disembarked and found the port to be a hustle of traders, the island having been carved into desperate plantations in the fertile spaces surrounding its singular mountain, the dormant volcano peak of Teide. A woman ground insects in a large mortar. Fruit sellers wandered among us with bunches of bright bananas. Madoc spoke to them in Spanish that was unaccented, apart from his welsh baritone. The woman grinding the insects pulled her red-dyed shawl around her shoulders, agreeing with him. "Si, una tormenta."

Captain Madoc was keen to reach the Plaza de Toros. This was the bullring of Santa Cruz, and Richardson and I accompanied him, assured of a spectacle. From the outside it was a tall white walled arena shaded by palms, a plain kind of Colosseum. Posters advertising the bullfights were pasted inside the shaded stucco alcoves. Birds gathered in the Moorish arches. Inside the great ring, tiered rows of benches circled upwards toward the gallery roof that shaded the highest positions. Hundreds of locals were already inside, talking animatedly and fanning themselves with newspapers.

A squat figure in denim navigated the spectators, carrying a crate of bottled beers, cheerfully snatching money from any patrons who raised their handkerchiefs for his custom. The three of us attracted his attention and paid him. He kept his beer cold by bedding it in wet straw, and he bit the caps off with chipped yellow teeth. Thankfully, Richardson managed to interrupt him before he could open our bottles for us by waving his steel bottle opener ostentatiously, while Captain Madoc in his Swansea Spanish called out: "No la boca! No la boca!" The beer was good and the Plaza de Toros was festive. We had cheap seats in the direct blast of the sun, but our view of the sand ring over the wooden barricade was close range. The surface of the bullring had been raked meticulously—the golden lens of it reflecting eddies of heat. "Maybe that storm of yours will hurry up, Madoc," Richardson groaned. A group of spectators quite near to us began singing together, tilting their beers to their mouths in unison. They looked to have come straight from the harbor market, sweating and soiled with their work.

I said: "What's that they're singing, Madoc?"

He listened for a moment. "Oh, something about the Devil living in their volcano, back there, and how he pisses on the hot slopes because he is incarnated as a black dog. When the lava steams from his piss, he can't see his way to the Plaza de Toros."

"That's good," Richardson and I agreed.

When the shanty ended, all of us that were seated well enough to hear it rose to applaud. The beer seller cried with laughter, chewing off more beer bottle caps and handing drinks to the singers. They wiped the bottles they had earned with their sleeves. Gradually, the odor of the bulls reached us from their tight cages. Picadors rode about, their lances decorated with pennants showing the colors and arms of the Islands.

*Dynamite under the tracks—the darkening ground—brass wire—*Finally, as the afternoon came, a bull moved slowly into the shadows close to the wooden walls, eyeing the glittering youth who stood poised in the vortex of the ring. The great crest of muscle—that I learned the matadors call the *morrillo*—that ran from its shoulder blades through its neck and permitted it to toss and thrash its gruesome minatory horns was wickedly overdeveloped. The bull circled back to the entrance of its prison, a pair of doors blocked with iron bars, daubed with wine and old blood. This bull, we were told, through Madoc, was abnormal. It was rare for any bull to leave the ring, yet this one had killed three youthful matadors, and in some parody of honor had been permitted to live and fight again. It mangled the picadors beneath their streaming bloody horses. It disemboweled the bravest of Tenerife in their suits of light, and tossed them as shredded rags over its bible-black shoulders. Some called for it to be withdrawn from the circuit, and others for it to be shot. Always, it left the ring wreathed in blood and surrounded by an awful silence, broken only by wails of mourning. It was a compelling horror, like an ancient nightmare that had broken into the universe of flesh and bone, and was doing its work. Its violence had inverted the sacraments of the bullring. It embodied centuries of catholic fear bound in one awful form, something grotesque and intractably human seemed to push from within its hide, and roared in sheets of flame from its tar-black eyes. It was rumored that on certain nights, certain moons and certain feast days, its eyes would turn blue and tender, much as those a man might have, a strange accursed blue filled with sorrow and self-pity. Perhaps, the aficionados said, that blue was seen by the matadors it killed, in the final moment before it cocked its wicked horns into their groins, ripping out arteries, a fatal knowledge shared in the ferocious heat of the Plaza. I regarded its thick scars. The beast cried in almost human despair. Tears flowed from its eyes and mucous glistened from its sorrowful muzzle. It flicked its horns in shallow arcs, still seemingly compelled by an instinct, against its will. Its tongue was a vivid pink. I hated to see it die.

"It's a medieval way to die," Richardson mused.

"The Catholics love it," I said, because the bull is Jesus Christ. This basin we're in is an inverted Calvary. We're present at the deception, the scourging, the spearing and the crucifixion. That's a red Roman robe, and also the tearing of the veil. Bullfighting is an *auto da fe*."

"You're not Catholic, are you, Kurtz?"

I shook my head, sipping my beer, chilled no longer. "It'll be a new century in a few years. It seems to me that the more modern we become, the more desperately the devils protest. It will be too late for them soon, and they know it."

"Is that why you're going to the Congo, then, Boyo? To preserve your devils?"

"Really, I'm not sure, Madoc."

But I saw it then. I had been Cruelty's Passenger for such a long time. That was what I was—somewhere between my origin and my destination—*A Passenger To Cruelty.*

Dakar was our next port, two days later. Dakar is a fang that hangs off the edge of the continent. We did not disembark and Richardson changed our orders with regard to commodities. We only took on board certain preserved foods that were supplied in tins or bottles, nothing porous, wrapped in paper, or in sacks, no open fruit or vegetables. There was a sickness in Dakar, and we could not risk contamination. Through Madoc's telescope, I saw Negroid figures vomiting and crawling along the wharf, as the legionnaires rowed supply boats out to us. The French appeared sullen and worried. I was disappointed not to have been able to set foot on African soil, albeit a Gallic commune under a pall of nausea.

At the Victoria Hotel in Free Town, Sierra Leone, they served quinine with everything. The imported European waiters were a disheveled crew, their formal black suits shiny from the dirty perspiration they were obliged to wipe from their faces with their sleeves, because there were no more clean handkerchiefs to mop it. Their shirts were stained with sweat and soup. The passengers of the *Mandingo* seemed to be the only guests they had seen in years. Spiders crawled on the motionless ceiling fans because the generator ran only erratically. Through the humidity, there was a tangible ripple of panic that overflowed through the damp bedrooms and ran out through cracks in the murky windowpanes. The hotel served wild game under dull silver cloches. The unshaven British waiter who attended me had no tray to carry drinks upon. I was handed a gin and tonic in a sticky tumbler. I smoked a cigarette and watched the waiters and servants move languidly between the rooms, leaning against the ebony piano in the sun lounge as though the Victoria was a travesty of tropical gentlemen's club laboring under typhoid. I was informed that there should be ivory ashtrays, but that Company men returning to Europe had stolen them.

From beneath this glass-roofed conservatory, with its exotic plants, vines groping through the white floor tiles, I passed through a set of unhinged French doors, out, alone, into my first African evening. As the lighthouse turned in the bay, I drifted like a ghost over the veranda, into the embrace of a green wilderness. I stood in the tall grass beyond the view of the gaudily decaying hotel, suddenly unable to see the revolving beam that warned ships off the reefs. The jungle extended itself toward me, the verdant ectoplasm of millions of years fusing bone marrow and chlorophyll, as though it had been waiting patiently outside me, and dormant within me. The wide leaves dripped time. Slowly, with infinite care, I reached my fingers into it like a blind man standing before the noise of a green waterfall. A shockwave of primordial communication swept ahead of me, mysterious impressions of voices, serpentine, massive, a great swell of sympathy. All the tender obscenity of Nature cried out at my first touch. We two were innocent of one another. And like a narcotic dream, all that I desired was to penetrate deeper, to put hard edges on these mere impressions, to inhabit them. From the fronds and tendrils came an eerie shrieking. Bizarre sonorous howls exploded from the emerald canopy of the trees. Their branches rubbed and creaked in the watery breeze. As I stood, enraptured by the weird cacophony of the forest, the immeasurable snare of a dark geography whispered beneath it: *Ssssooo—you've—come—hooome—at—laasssst—*

Off the Liberian Coast, the next afternoon, sharks were sighted. One of the Durban prospectors, a skinny mercenary type named Van Broekhuizen took up a position at the bow of the steamer, taking shots at them with his service revolver. The slate fins came in ellipses about the ship as Van Broekhuizen wasted some of his rations, shaking tins of pilchards out into the ocean as bait. Eventually, Captain Madoc came down and humiliated him, and this arrogant skeleton in khaki retreated to his bunk to sleep off his hangover. The sharks seemed to relish the pilchards, at least, and none appeared wounded. I remained on the port side, watching the tropical coastline, thinking of that fringe of jungle beyond the Victoria Hotel. It was the first nervous touch of a lover. I studied the estuaries of immense channels, imagining how they traced inland under sap trees, brackish waters knotted with crocodiles, haunted by luminous birds. I was impatient to be on land again. In contrast, Richardson, since Dakar and the sight of more Negroes in their death throes, had become morbidly reluctant to consider going ashore. "The scene of the crime," he called it. As we rounded the coast and the *Mandingo* turned due east toward Sekondi, we sat in striped deckchairs, eating oranges, tossing the peel over the railings into the waves. I noticed that Richardson refused to raise his eyes toward the mangroves and golden sand bars. Instead, he fixed his gaze conspicuously upon the fruit in his lap and the glass of burgundy wobbling on the deck beside his right plimsoll. When he lifted it to his mouth, the tremens of his guilt infected him again. Derelict Dutch forts interrupted the tree line. Something white the size of a man drifted past the ship, the corpse of a Company man wrapped in muslin. Richardson was inconsolable.

"What about Fresleven?" I asked him. "Why did you want to know about him, in particular?"

Richardson shrugged. "In truth, I never really knew the man. That was just second-hand, reputation and rumor from Madoc." A little wine stained his jacket.

"Chinese whispers. What was Madoc's interest?"

"Madoc brought him down, took him to the bullfights, showed him the slave stations in the Bight, all that. It's the routine, part of the Grand Tour, you might say. Actually, Madoc wasn't overly impressed with Fresleven, to be frank. He thought him petty, 'like an officious blonde policeman.' But, Madoc did admit that he got that ivory down the river regular as clockwork."

"Do you imagine that's the best way?" I asked.

Richardson coughed on his wine, turning to me and smiling. "That's a funny question, coming from a Company man!"

Although I could not have voiced it then, I think that I must have known already that time was running out for the Congo.

Protruding streambed—cannibal children—lungfish—Madoc navigated the *Mandingo* to the south after the hard surf of the Bight of Benin, white breakers crashing over splintered slave pontoons. We were sailing away from the Gold Coast. I remember it as a wild and haunted place, with several imperial powers succumbing to the overwhelming claustrophobia of the tides and the cannibal aggression of the forests. Between the palms, hollow churches disintegrated like Aztec ruins. Close to one of the bloodstained docks, a bell tower sounded in the wind, a soft, low knell of mourning. We were closing in on the Equator, steaming between volcanic islands that had once been great western peaks, before the ocean flooded the plains between them and the edge of the continent. There were many occasions when our ship could only be perceived as a splinter in this immensity, when the sea appeared monolithic in its surface. We became a filing of iron between magnetisms too distant to be comprehended, shaking on a sea of stalemate.

Richardson despaired, desiring nothing less than to wheel the ship about and to return at full steam to England, without ever reaching the Congo. The sun whipped him and the stars were salt in his wounds. Perhaps it was because I pitied him that I began to avoid him during the final leagues of the voyage. Something informed me that pity is a finite and ever-diminishing currency. Watching him shuddering in the twilight, I knew that Richardson had gone far beyond the point of total expenditure. Now, he was mawkish with lack. The absence of genuine pity demanded a parody in the cold void where it had been. This was your father's house, where he sought out my soul. This is why he paid off the Company to grant me a Station commission, to make me a captain. It served both his contempt and his disingenuousness. He wanted me out of London. You must know this by now. And I, in my summer ruin, exploited his hatred of me as another means of disappearing.

At last, the Atlantic was tinged with roiling sediment in a broad arc that billowed out for a great distance outside of the estuary. Long before we reached our anchor site, the sea change was observable as a kaleidoscope of yellow ochre, dun clouds, and glittering golden currents. All the deep blue and moss green colors of the water were blasted away by the wash of this African river dirt. It was as though, hundreds of miles upriver, a vast cannibal cauldron had been spilled, and this was the endless broth of so many dead men. The ship steamed as if through a brown ocean of sand dunes, and this was the true sign that we were drawing in on the Congo. Watching the verdant coast, a void appeared suddenly in that horizon where the trees receded and the river burst out. We put in at Banana, an outcropping port on the northern side of the estuary, where a crane bearing large woven baskets would swing us ashore in sweating clusters of men. The baskets, suspended from their boom by strong cables and winched by shining Negroes, were similar to those carried beneath hot air balloons. They creaked as we hung over the dockside. I shared my transport with a middle-aged missionary, and a young putty-faced accountant—neither of which have I set eyes upon again in the two years that I have occupied my station.

Impressions of Africa, of the incalculable Congo, are naturally disordered. It is, quite simply, too wild, too excessive in attitude, with the vines, the rocks, the creatures that have swollen out of the ground and the sheets of heat and water. The violence of the outpour as it nears the ocean is like Scylla unraveling, tendrils of foam and mud. The European, or any non-Native is cast into the most sublime confusion. I have come to regard it as a rite of passage: if he resists or objects to this disorientation, then he is damned, and will discover the secret cause of his death almost as he disembarks his steamer. The impress of this continent is exceeding heavy. To survive more than a year, it demands a form of surrender to a prologue of dirt and a future of grime—*no knowledge of the face of the earth, no account of time, no arts, no letters, no society, and which is worst of all, continual fear and danger of violent death, and the life of man, solitary, poor, nasty, brutish, and short*—The boom of an ancient percussion beats you upon your breast as soon as you admit that there is no returning from this point. Even if the husk of the body exits for some purple squalor in Chatham, Liverpool, or Brussels, the spirit—or something like it—remains tethered to a totem like Saint Sebastian full of arrows.

Mami Wata—the station in coils—At Banana, we stretched our legs while some of the cargo was winched onto the spit by the natives of the north lip of the river, singing their eerie music while a Frenchman strode about them, dressed in pale khaki, with a perforated white Stanley cap tilting on his brow. The Englishman held a whip in his sinister hand and he supervised in only the most cursory manner. I think that he merely wished to use the whip. Yet the black men winched efficiently, the tar of their long limbs smothering the mechanism and the nets. I think that perhaps the young putty-faced accountant remained there in Banana, working in one of the stilted buildings, sweating over tedious ledgers. I can picture him, tallying tusks and corpses, regretting himself. The crates and chests were taken off to improve the *Mandingo*'s draught, permitting it to pass over the dorsal sandbar that precedes the outpost at Boma. This delay was necessary and routine. Madoc had suffered it a dozen times, smoking on his bridge. It was frustrating. I was full of agitation, anticipating a new station in a new darkness. Banana had the stamp of the new upon it. It also appeared improvised and fragile, as I would learn, much of the colonization effort would seem. A conflict of national and company flags asserted itself over the red roof tiles of the houses and the echoing hotel, almost empty. I went back aboard our steamer, now sitting higher in the current. The skeletal wreckage of a paddleboat drifted alongside us as we rejoined the main channel; a half-submerged box of dynamite went with it. Less encumbered, transitioning from the Atlantic Ocean water into the Congo, I perceived a subtle shift in the ship's engines, as though even the machinery would function differently in the compass of Africa.

"That's what they call Fetish Rock." The phosphor spark of a match and a troubled voice announced Richardson's presence beside me at the rail, under the stars. I remember that I thought that out there in the white strokes of moonlight, the rock wasn't much to look at. "Madoc says we lay anchor there." It was on the south bank, a modest escarpment. "He says it's our first place of genuine danger."

"What does he mean by that?"

Richardson inhaled slowly before going on: "The rock is haunted. It's where the niggers throw their babies, and the boys that will never become warriors, off into the river to drown. And if it was daylight, and thank God it's not, we'd see the place the cannibals stake human skins out to dry in the sun. I mean: do you *smell* that?"

I confessed that I could not, straining to make out the lineaments of the outcrop.

"Long pig and fresh blood. I know the scent of blood," he said.

All that I could smell was the pleasant smoke of his navy tobacco. I reminded Richardson that perhaps he might have waited in the hotel at Banana, and not come further in. He shivered visibly at the suggestion.

"Kurtz . . . Why would I leave the ship?"

Richardson handed me a cigarette paper and opened his tin of leaf. I took a pinch and began rolling it. "Madoc is winding you up, you understand, Richardson?"

"This bloody continent is winding me up. It's thick with bad memories. Wicked juju." A funnel of bats rose from a hollow in the rock. "Why did you come here, Kurtz? What's in it for you?"

"Well," I said, "when I was a boy, I would imagine an endless war between progress and phantoms." I dragged on my cigarette, and Richardson scoffed quietly, unsure of my sincerity, I think. "That's what I came here to witness."

"The world's not as poetic as that, son. During the war with the Zulus—"

"Isn't it?" I cut him off. "Does it matter what you call the antagonists?"

"I've killed. Why on earth would you want to see any of that carnage?"

"I don't," I said. "I want to cut through it all, really, like the walls of a hurricane, right into the absolute stillness and silence inside the vortex. There, I intend to sit it out. Don't get me wrong—this isn't a journey of exploration for me. It's one of abandonment, to claim the throne at the center of the world, and to *abdicate* at one and the same moment."

"I don't think I'm detective enough to follow you, Kurtz."

"You should stay on the ship if you want. And I hope and trust that you will return to England, happily, Richardson."

Removing his white steward's jacket and hanging it on the railing, he asked me: "Where is your family?"

I shook my head.

We did not speak any more that night before retiring. We smoked our cigarettes and listened to the water slapping against the hull and Fetish Rock. The next day, we crossed the sandbar to Boma.

Mboze's pregnant belly turning white—albescence—murder— I believe that it was early October 1889 when we moored against the metal pier. At Boma, we had steamed fifty nautical miles from the spit of Banana. Here, in a downpour, I met Janssens in his whitewashed wooden pavilion, the residence of Governor General. Impressive verandas scrolled away from the high entry staircase. Streams of brown rainwater ran beneath the main floor, which was raised up on blue-painted wooden pillars, bolted with rusting iron. Janssens had a short beard, spreading out in two horizontal tangles, so that he resembled something between a down-at-heel Belgian gentleman and a hammerhead shark. His breast was adorned with polished medals, and he wore a bright yellow sash of satin over his blue coat. We sat outside, beneath the tight thatch of a balcony, drinking decanted claret from crystal glasses.

"Your father-in-law spoke so very convincingly of you," he explained. "The Brussels Office got word to me on one of the Durban postal ships, before they ever had a chance to meet you in person." Janssen thumbed through some papers of rain-blurred ink, murmuring rhetorically. "Educated at Oxford, excellent—fluent in languages, good—and one of the Prince of Wales' Royal 12th Lancers—"

Drinking on that terrace, I further understood the extent to which your father was willing to embellish my imaginary past to get me out of England, for our engagement to end in malaria. I shrugged my shoulders, resignedly. "I can't claim that I was much of a cavalryman, Sir."

"Modesty. Discipline. These are attributes, particularly in this place . . . and a classicist, in study. You've read Livy, I presume. No horses for cavalrymen here, I'm afraid. They die. They drown, they disease, they die. Hannibal was right with his elephants. More claret?" Janssens clapped his hands and his boy came emerged from the shadows to serve us. He appeared to be about eight years old, and there was, I thought, a decent chance that Janssens' prefecture was the cause of his orphaning. I imagined the boy's parents bleeding in a pretty grove under a yellow-starred flag. The boy poured the drinks without trembling, and Janssens smiled at him, saying, "Good boy. Well done." He was genial, Janssens. He instructed me about Matadi, where I would call next, and told me that I could get a head start by not waiting for Madoc and my steamer, but by going earlier on one of the smaller steamboats. Matadi would be the last outpost before the rapids would force me inland. He spoke also of the perils of his own post, as he slashed the watery air with his fly swatter. "They . . . many agents slip into what I call *The Boma Coma*. I have about a dozen men in the hospital here, locked in coma, right now as we sit here imbibing our hygiene."

"What is it?"

"We can't say, exactly."

I thought of the blue uniformed men I had seen along the pier, in the artificial streets, smoking outside the orphanage and the jail. I imagined them collapsing like piles of rags into impenetrable slumber . . . pristine, buttoned-up, well-drilled agents drifting into living death. This spectral continent had its way—miniscule bacteria wiping out the avant-garde invaders.

"We do our best to get them out, but they rarely survive the crossing beyond the Tropic of Cancer. They are buried at sea."

The steamer that would transport me to Matadi, the final point after which upstream navigation becomes impossible for some distance, came in and my belongings and supplies were transferred across the pier from the *Mandingo*. Negroes in stained loincloths bore my sea chests upon their shoulders. Their skins were pocked and etched, the black rope of their muscles twisting and coiling in the effort. Janssens had explained that his boy and many of the porters had been brought down from the slave pontoons at Sekondi. I judged that the one who worked with my white-stenciled luggage was of a lighter, angular Moroccan caste. What was it I witnessed in the bondage of all this negritude—resignation, patience, or absolute abjection? I could not tell, then. I thought of the subjugation and subordination that my own father demanded, advancing across the globe, a hungry paternal evil. I walked in the footsteps of his dominion, and extended them, tracking and printing them upon this weird iron pier, on the banks of an infested tract, thousand of miles away. It was some provincial cruelty writ large. Before evil is outrun, it swallows thousands of innocents in the pursuit.

The steamer was a boxy construction, flying the blue flag and yellow star of the Force Publique. It was called the *Roi de Belges*. My luggage was lowered into it from the pier where it was received by more laboring slaves, gritting their teeth and sweating under the burden, swathing me in the funk of their bodies. The more I appraised the boat, the greater of a shambles it appeared. Sections of the decks had been patched with warping plywood, and canopy was ragged toward the stern where the paddle dripped weeds into the river. I watched the shadowed hull of the *Mandingo* shrink into the distance as we travailed upstream. The banks steepened, grew taller, an opaque tangle of mangroves and large sap trees. A verdant canyon began to assert itself about us, as the low hills pushed up into angular downs. This is when I met Fresleven.

Letting one of his boys steer the boat, he sought me out. He was a big man, Viking blonde in the suede fuzz of hair that he kept. He had not shaved in a week, I estimated. His shirt was soaked with perspiration. He extended his massive hand to me. When I took it, and we shook, his grip was uncommonly slight. His blue eyes were rimmed red, irritated by the outpour of his own salts. "I hear that you've been assigned to the inner station. I'm pleased to encounter you, Mr. Kurtz, even if it comes a week too late for the man you're replacing." His accent was as mild as his grip.

"Your reputation reached me on the Atlantic," I said, pleased to find him.

At this, he laughed, a quiet soprano cascade. "Ha! Which one? Good Fresleven or Bad Fresleven?"

I had to laugh with him.

"Are you hungry? We'll fry some buffalo on the boiler. It's good."

I assented and he whistled to one of his boys to begin the cooking. Then, I asked Fresleven, "How long have you been here, really?"

"Not long. I want to stick it out for a couple of years, but I know it's unlikely. I want a pension to see me to America."

"What do you make of your crew?"

"Honestly, I like them, but they bicker."

"With you?"

"Of course not. They know I can chicotte or kill them in a heartbeat. No, it's in the way they have to adjust to our ways, our hierarchies. They don't understand enough. For instance, I can make one my boiler man, and another my tea boy, and neither will understand who outranks the other."

"I suppose I might be at a loss, were I in their skins."

"Now, *that* they comprehend: the White's untouchable." Fresleven patted his hip, where I noted his revolver in its canvas holster. "A spear isn't much to a bullet. You should enjoy this stretch. You're in for a savage march after Matadi."

She visited me again, last night. The wire wool of her pubis, the ermine lips swallowing me, her bronze hips washing me in her tide. I spent myself in her. I sucked the rims of her scars, tasting the salt on her spine. When I awoke, the incubus had gone, leaving an animal scent on my fingers. Your image in my mind was obliterated.

*Calabash gourds filled with blood—stripped vegetation— palaku marimbas—*What I recall of arriving at Matadi was the gratuitous conflict of sound, between the natural and the unnatural. First, there was the incessant roar of the rapids above us, the vertiginous cataracts that writhe and screw from a relatively narrow point through the unwinding chasm upstream to Stanley Pool. Within that, however, I also knew the source of that case of dynamite that had floated past our steamer back at Banana. The percussion of these explosives inland penetrated the harsh wash of the falls with staccato pulses. Beneath these I heard also the relatively feeble reports of gunfire. This parallax of noise was another aspect of the disorder of the Congo and its disturbing effect upon the senses. It drowned introspection and reasoning thought. The sights of the Matadi pier and the expanse beyond were dislocated from their meaning and morality by the deafening echoes of Progress.

My luggage was brought off the *Roi de Belges* by four blacks. Fresleven did not linger at Matadi, but directed me to the station of the Company's Chief Accountant. Fresleven assured me that my cargo would remain safe upon the jetty, until either the Chief Accountant's boys or members of what would be my own caravan could collect it. According to the Dane, there was no theft at Matadi. I walked the dirt track uphill toward the station, tempted to cover my ears with my hands, yet mindful of appearing as nervous or unaccustomed, as I was. To the west, another explosion was followed by the sound of screaming and falling trees.

Shrapnel of dirt and stones strafed the surface of the water, as I turned my face away from the dynamiting. Fresleven sounded his steamer's whistle. It was like a toy in a storm, and the last I saw of him was this image of a lost Viking figure shaking his fist at the pillar of smoke swiveling up out of the jungle.

Turning inland again, the din of the rapids still pressing on me, I saw a gang of Negroes leaning on shovels at the lip of a small crater. There must have been six or seven of them conscripted there, chained together in iron collars that drew rings of blood from their throats when they walked or worked out of rhythm. As I took them in, another emerged from the broad shadow of a palm. This one was not enchained, but wore with European formality the uniform of the Company. It was in his hand that I first witnessed the chicotte—a six-foot whip wound from hippopotamus hide—in use. The diggers had not seen, nor heard him approaching their flank, and he lashed their ribs and shoulder with a savage disinterest, as though he were directing stubborn beasts. The whip splitting their skins became merely another of the dissonant percussions of the station. The diggers mouthed their agonies silently, as he set about them, even as they shoveled heavy soil back into the hole. Stepping closer, I understood that it was a grave. Then, there was another explosion. It washed through the trees, throwing dirt upon all of us. I saw about me that there were several fresh bulges in the ground. These crater-graves were meant for more than one man. As soon as this one was filled, another would be ordered, and it would await its accountant's quota of decimated men. None of the beetle-black men paid any attention to me. I might as well have been a ghost, drifting through the carnage of an exhausted battle, resented and accepted in one mind. As I neared the edge where they labored, I could see into the hollow. Partly obscured with dirt was a wicked tangle of corpses. The gang kept shoveling, still ignoring me.

I stared downward, dumbstruck, upon the soft wreckage of so many human beings. They resembled some orgy of trunks and rubber stopped in time, their eyes fixed, dilated, the shocked sclera turned to a dull ivory. Some of them appeared to have fallen into an exhausted sleep, while others were mutilated into nightmarish deportment. Wrists without hands projected from the pile. Palates without lower jaws gaped against the mud sliding into the pit. Either they had been executed or they had been blown to smithereens by the dynamite detonating through the forest. The corpses had been dusted with quicklime, and that ate into the open wounds, enlarging them, as though the whitening skins were peeling open, to let out the fizzing flesh beneath.

*The cicatrice on her skin—walking with a bamboo cane— ankle stumps in ferns—*What sense of shame and horror I am able to imprint here is surely a superimposition of my current mind upon the past. As I said, I was then operating under the somnambulistic and deadening spell of the Matadi station. When I say that I *understood* that the pit was a grave, all that I can mean is that I *saw* that it was a grave. Viscerally, morally, even intellectually, I understood nothing, yet. Things shifted in an affectless cacophony, living things, dead things, all that quivered and bled at the margins—The cannibal mouths of the diggers moved as broad pink-black diaphragms. The chicotte flew in sparks of sunlight. The trees swayed. Beneath the falling earth, the corpses were pleading with a narrowing sky—

Higher up, during an intermission in the detonations, I came to the premises of the Chief Accountant. The white-washed sidings of his strange villa were capped by a recently restored thatch roof, where scores of small vibrant birds now congregated, funneling down from the blue spaces above. He opened his slatted door on witnessing my approach. To the right of his building was a shelter where he piled ivory. I hesitated, regarding the long bent cones of the tusks. Then I heard his wooden door slap closed behind him. He maintained an aspect that reminded me of any Limehouse dandy, back in London, although the pose appeared some-what alien to him. Dressed in a pristine cream suit and shining oxblood cavalry boots, he moved pretentiously, a false grace propelling him between two rows of vermillion orchids. His hair was brilliant and shoe polish-black—he either colored it, or remained out of the bleach of the sun always. Halfway toward me, he raised what I had taken to be a walking cane, and the green panels of a parasol burst open over his head. "I'm Rommel, and you must be Kurtz, of London, or Paris, or the Ghetto," he said, trailing off, twisting the edge of his moustache with his free hand. I felt the wax on his fingers when we shook.

The problem with Rommel was that he was snide. He was the type of man who seeks to radiate superiority from the vacant tube where his spine ought to be. Therefore, he was superficially offhand with newcomers and associates alike. I noticed that the flies that infested the station were fond of the pomade he used upon his hair, but they were no inconvenience to his self-regard. He spoke little to me that did not betray some barb of bitterness that he supposed would undermine and reduce me. Such was his disinterested aggression, the insinuating violence of the bureaucrat who had found the final rung on his own ladder. That night, while he worked on his ledgers, I read by candlelight beside the smeared window of his office. Large moths fluttered against the glass. There was nowhere else for me to wait, except for the ratty divan he kept there. Through the gray wings of the insects, the turbulent impression of the rapids washed through the pane. Rommel said, "Want a cigarette? I doubt that you've ever tasted this brand before." Then: "So many people pretend to read these days." These things he murmured theatrically from the side of his mouth as though I were a dumb actor at whom the entire jungle was laughing. He irritated me, intensely. "What exactly are you so buried in, over there?" I held up the cover of the book for him to see, not wishing to be drawn into any discourse with him than was required to get me out of Matadi in the coming days. He was not a man that one could learn anything from. He was cold and arrogant. Rommel squinted at my book, clasping his tongue between his teeth, shaking his head, deliberately uncomprehending. Finally, I answered him.

"It's a book of poems. My father presented it to me."

"What a beneficent old Jew he must have been. *Une Saison . . . d'Enfer . . .* Sounds exceptionally average."

I gave him nothing more. I let another twenty minutes elapse in silence. Rommel was deep into his accounts, finally ignoring me. He would slip his fountain pen in and out of the ivory penholder that he balanced over his right ear. The only sounds now were the shifting of his papers over his long-legged mahogany desk, his intermittent *tuts* of contempt for whatever calculations he had before him, and the moths at the window, and the constant valedictions of the irreducible river to the endless night. Quietly, I rose from the divan. His back was to me. I stood waiting for his tongue's next click of complaint. When it came, only seconds later, I took him. Before he could protest, my right forearm was under his chin, choking him. My left hand gripped a slick clot of his hair, wrenching his scalp. I remember the sound of his hair ripping from his skin, as I adjusted my fingers for more. There was a thin bubbling from his windpipe. His arms flailed weakly, his fingers shaking and clawing. When I felt him close to unconsciousness, I released his throat, and with both hands I smashed his head forward and down upon his desk. He spilled inanimately from his stool to the wooden floor, leaving a stamp of blood on his report. I stood over him, and switched off his lamp. There was only my candle by the window. He vomited upon his pale clothes, rolling and kicking like an animal. I jabbed his ribs with my boot. "Don't try to debase me, Rommel. I'm going in further, deeper than anyone else! Slight me again and I'll kick out your teeth and pay your gravediggers with them."

Within me, my blood gave off a rotten odor.

I had smelled it before.

Outside, I found an empty hut and sat on the floor inside it. There was no furniture. The door hung on one corroded hinge. There was a small window that let in a shaft of moonlight. On the bare floor, I made out some simple tools, a trowel and a pair of pliers. A dented tin of herring that had been cleaned out by ants had been tossed into a corner. I found myself thinking of the crones at the Brussels office, knitting their black wool, and the feeling of Severijns' fingers manipulating and tracing my skull like any other specimen. Is that what I was? A porcelain head, stuck on a shelf, staring at another just like me that was annotated with calligraphy where I was blank. Then I was a new crucified moth under glass, a curious species, nothing more. Then I was an elephant bleeding from the holes where my tusks had been. The words I had spat out at Rommel as he lay wounded beneath me seemed to echo around the hut, fleeting through my head in my mother's voice, my father's voice, and every accent of Europe, *going in further, deeper than anyone else!* I was anything but a man. I saw one of the old women standing up from her knitting and crossing the marble floor in her widow dress. I think that I opened my mouth to scream, yet none came out, only a distant whine that I would not have believed belonged to me were it not for the ache in my larynx. Kicking the door closed, with what presence I maintained, I reached out across the dirt floor, my hands scrambling for the trowel. The old woman in my mind reached for the venetian blinds. In horror, I looked at the shaft of moonlight. I put the filthy wooden handle of the trowel in my mouth and bit down hard upon it. Even as I did so, black stripes fell across the silvery brightness of the window—

In the morning, I went to see Rommel. I told him that I was sorry. It was the truth. When I moved, he flinched. It must have been how my father felt, sometimes, when remorse came to him. How does a criminal remind his victim that even he was a man, once? How did my mother forgive him? He wasn't wearing a shirt, one of his boys having taken it to launder on a clean rock. Rommel's white body was covered with red bites and the angry mounds of stings. He was pulling at one with a pair of silver tweezers. "Let me help you," I said, taking them from him. Rommel looked at me with the perplexed expression of a dog beaten by the hand that feeds it. His blue eyes were filled with thwarted yearning. A gentle scent of cologne and calamine bloomed from his pores. As I put my fingers upon him, as tenderly as I could, what had been a nervous shivering calmed to a statuary trance. I extracted the hair-like barbs from his pallid flesh, and dropped them into porcelain shaving dish. I must have accounted fifty black stings from the ledger of his body. I saw the sheen of tears over his slightly bulbous eyes. When we had finished, Rommel rolled his bony shoulders and poured a pitcher of water over himself, his white trousers becoming transparent under it, the scarab whorls of his groin showing in the slatted sunlight. His lips parted where his thoughts pressed outwards. There was a timid knock at the door. Rommel didn't speak. I said, "Come in." It was the boy with Rommel's shirt. It was dazzlingly clean, draped over a stripped branch like a flag. Light seemed to come out of it. Abruptly, I recognized the boy behind it. It was the one with the chicotte who had so savagely punished the gravediggers in their iron collars. Wordlessly, Rommel took the shirt and dressed, although his skin was still damp. The boy in the blue uniform retreated from the office. I saw his whip coiled at his side, held by a thong to one of his empty belt loops. The door closed behind him, and I crossed to the window by the divan to watch him descend. There was a bottle of whisky on the divan, and I knew that Rommel had slept with it.

"Can you stand another drink?"

"Yes. Please." He finished buttoning his shirt.

"That one," I said, "is vicious."

"I'm quite sure that you're right. He's an ordinal case, I'm afraid. I keep trying. I should take his rank and privileges away from him. But, honestly, I am petrified of what might replace him. It gets worse, every time. The cruelty of that one will only be eclipsed by his successor. It's human nature. Well, perhaps it is. Human nature no longer applies out here, in here." Later, I would learn that the boy took the shirt to a woman who may have been his wife to do the cleaning. She did not approach the office, unless she was absolutely compelled to.

"How long has he been in charge of them?"

"Eight weeks. He's quite young, actually—I think fifteen or sixteen years old. Thereabout."

"What happened to his predecessor?"

"He murdered him."

"With a shovel." I knew how it must have been.

"Of course," Rommel admitted. "It will surely happen again, in its own time. Poor beggar."

"Perhaps he should come with me. What are we doing here, Rommel?"

The Chief Accountant stared at me from a prison of melancholy.

Connais-je encore la nature? Me connais-je?—Plus de mots. J'ensevelis les morts dans mon ventre. Cris, tambour, danse, danse, danse, danse! Je ne vois même pas l'heure où, les blancs débarquant, je tomberai au néant. Faim, soif, cris, danse, danse, danse, danse! Les blancs débarquent. Le canon! Il faut se soumettre au baptême, s'habiller, travailler. J'ai reçu au coeur le coup de la grâce. Ah! je ne l'avais pas prévu!

But, things were fixed between us. When my caravan arrived, Rommel watched from a distance, the shade of his parasol barely concealing the distended bruise on his forehead. He stood near the ivory shelter, the currency that he merely . . . counted. Perhaps, once or twice as he watched us gathering our load for the inland walk, a faint smirk deformed his mouth, imagining me dying on the trail, a spear in my gullet like a mast on my floating corpse. From the bottom of the hill, I waved and called up to him. "Be certain that you write with news, Rommel, if anything happens here." His vicious boy came with me.

There were sixty in our caravan, a vine-black snake stretching more than one hundreds yards in length. Vicious Boy asserted himself at the head of it, insinuating his way into the confidence of its leader, a half-caste named Johnny Malebo—at least, that is what he insisted on being called, now that he was a Company agent. Vicious Boy was all smiles at his side, recognizing in the division of Malebo's genes the transitional potential of hybridity and the modern prototype of paternity. He was somewhat in awe. Malebo had been incubated in a slave woman's womb, yet his agency had not been denied him. His father—I would learn—was a Yorkshire man, a miner who had advised on the geology of the region twenty years ago. Now that I saw what the poor devils had to bear through the resisting jungle, upon their heads and shoulders, in calloused hands, our enterprise struck me as obscene, decadent, and yet, wholly insufficient to the moment. The Negroes buckled under large crates, steamer chests, ammunition boxes and caches of rifles, bottles of champagne in wicker baskets, canned goods, medicines—in all, thousands of pounds divided into roughly fifty-pound burdens. The march alongside the cataracts would take two weeks, more than two hundred miles, covering barely two miles in an hour. Though the trail was established, the wilderness poured back into the route, hell-bent on reclaiming the hollows from man. It seemed only right, since this absurd caravan was chiefly for my benefit, for me to keep up with Johnny Malebo and Vicious Boy at the head of the line, clearing boughs and vines with flashing machetes. A railway was being built around the rapids, and we stepped along the skeletal track for the first few days. Slave gangs labored at it and envied us our passing. The scalding rails and broad sleepers were a mixed blessing for our caravan. As we hacked our way along the trail, Johnny Malebo and Vicious Boy conversed amiably in fragments of shared dialect. The sounds of it fascinated me, the low vowels that ran beneath the crashing of the flood. Soon, I found myself smiling when they smiled, and agreeing when they agreed, yet without comprehending a literal word of it—*Nzila kumbi—Nzadi Kongo—Mundelé*—Vicious Boy's smile lit by the sun—the sap dripping blades—the languorous heat and meanness of the trek—*railway—the Congo—white man*—

Floating islands—fetishes—plantains, and lime-leaf tea—Johnny Malebo's skin was a light coffee shade, sprayed with umber freckles and moles across the bridge of his broad nose and the high planes of his cheeks. His mouth, possibly, was of a more Caucasian type. The most remarkable aspects of the man were his copper-brown hair—still of the same wire wool appearance as any other Negro—and his mismatching eyes, scanning out from below the thick fold of his supraorbital ridge. I imagined Severijns molesting the poor man with rapacious scientific curiosity. Malebo's left eye was ebony, and his right was as blue as a sapphire. As he put it himself, his visage was a quiet civil war, fought to a stalemate. "Nobody wins," he said. I could but acquiesce to the evidence of his experience. His rank in the Company was both artificially elevated and suppressed by the novelty of his complexion. They had told him as much in Brussels. "I've never met another agent whose first thought was not the image of my mother and father as demons screwing in the tall grass." I reassured him that this was not so, in my case. He explained that he believed that his different eyes made antagonistic contact with the hemispheres of his brain. "But, my career as an Agent seems to have found its equilibrium between nigger and mundelé. So, I will not advance, but my betters do like to keep me close at hand, if *out here* counts as close at hand. I'm a totem, you see, an emblem."

"Of the future, surely," I suggested.

"Believe me, we will never belong, anywhere."

I didn't ask if he meant to include me in this *we*, because I wanted to believe that I was included and did not want this jungle spell to be broken. I rested my hand upon his sweat-soaked shoulder. I was pleased to be there.

Malebo removed his yellow-starred cap, wiping his brow with a handkerchief, and indicating Vicious Boy who had advanced several yards ahead of us along the scuffed track. "I think that it means a great deal to *him*, to be away from Matadi."

"And from Rommel?" I asked.

Malebo shrugged and put his cap back on, straightening the peak.

Watching Vicious Boy then, cavorting ahead of us with his vivid machete, brachiating under the low groves, I saw his youth blazing out of him. His blue coat was undone over his hairless and gleaming chest. He let out wild hoots and hyena cries as he went. He traipsed barefoot, and his trousers were rolled up over his knotted calves. The boy was compact and graceful, of medium height, the chicotte still swinging at his hip as he preceded us. Perhaps the pendulum would make him the future, a young, confident, golden king. When he returned and walked with us, he cast glances back down the length of the caravan. Ripples of anxiety passed through it, the black men like disturbed dominoes. Vicious Boy loved the power vested in him. I struggled to imagine him, if the Company had never come to Africa. I thought of the conscripted shadows behind us, singing their melancholy music under the brassy ring of the sun. Certainly, I had heard, and seen in Gibraltar, that they even enslaved one another, even before the Europeans arrived. In the pre-colonial age, anything could be currency. The colonial age narrowed the gauge of currency—and within that was the irony that for all of this stolen flesh to become valuable, it had first of all to be rendered worthless. The immensity of the waste choked me for a moment, before a blood-chilling scream erupted from the caravan, quite close behind us. One of the men had stumbled from the pathway. He was caught beneath the netting of his cargo, and was struggling to rise from a knot of vines. He was in a panic. Vicious Boy ran toward the hysterical form, calling out "J'ba fofi! J'ba fofi!" Suddenly, I saw that the things he hacked at with his machete were not brown creepers, but the angular legs of a gigantic arachnid. The man was caught in its hideously adhesive web, and was being bitten in the throat. He frothed and vomited, his limbs crabbing in on his torso until the paralysis of the venom stopped him dead. The spider was more than a yard across, a thick yellow poison oozing from the gashes cut into its fur. Vicious Boy was trembling when the half-caste and I reached his side. Malebo said something fierce to him, and he began to control his breathing again. As the two of them retrieved the luggage that the dead man had dropped, I heard the boy muttering "Kinkoló—"

"He thinks it was a spirit," Malebo explained.

"What spirit?"

"Perhaps . . . yours."

He had gone out there an insect, and returned a spider.

We buried the dead black and continued the journey. The caravan took up a solemn dirge as we tramped parallel to the waterfalls, making our way in a northeasterly direction. How much of the country was before us was incomprehensible. Vicious Boy was quiet for the remainder of the day and only began to revive when we were a few miles on. I offered him a shot of whisky. He took it, coughing as it went down. We laughed together as Malebo wagged a half-white finger in mock warning. I wondered if the boy possessed any inkling of the vastness of this place, where he was on the planet. That night, slightly drunk, I broke through to a clearing that afforded me a view of the river in all of its luminous spate under a full moon so argent and expanded in the hemisphere that it hovered barely above the canopy of the forest. Large bats traversed it. In the distance, I could see the Crystal Mountains with their weird auroras of quartz. It was the first time I had found to contemplate the seizure that had overtaken me during the night that I assaulted Rommel. I was profoundly afraid. What kink of my own blood was working in me, some tiny motes of syphilis swimming inside my veins like a shoal of hungry piranhas? Did it originate with my mother or with my father? Was it nothing of the sort, merely a psychosomatic spasm that came with the real knowledge of myself, that I was a brute? I was working up through the artery of Africa, boring right in to the center of the world. I swigged from the whisky bottle.

One should never underestimate the dangers inherent in the boiling tedium of rising and falling with a half-obliterated trail where flinty crags and ravines alternate with the soft grass and long lines of dust. Yet we had some luck with the rest of the walk, finding some sections of the trail less overgrown at the margins, wider and more sympathetic to our fatigue. Each caravan was sensibly obliged to scuff and prune the labyrinth for whoever would come behind, on the way in or out of the central station. Vicious Boy, still strutting ahead of us through his exhaustion, caught the first sign that the path was snaking closer to the river again. We heard him hollering back to us through a thinning copse. The insects increased and the earth showed moist and swamp-like to our left hand. We were to the southwest of Léopoldville and Kinshasa. At last, our caravan descended toward the open bank of sand. We were beyond the rapids. The rust brown waters had transformed to a dazzling peacock blue. We let the men lower their cargoes and clamber into it. They went jubilantly, splashing and ducking, while Johnny Malebo kept vigil with his rifle for any sign of crocodiles. The joys for these men were small and spare. I stripped off my clothes and went in with them. My skin reddened in the glare of the day, but at least I managed to wash the stink from my flesh. I waded there, one white body surrounded by what might have constituted an entire tribe of lethal warriors. Here, I was unafraid. The scintillating rays of the sun returned from the blue-green angles of the water. Vicious Boy swam toward me, his white grin threading through the film of it. He held a gaping flatfish in his hand. I plunged under the surface of the Congo, forgetting myself in the cool current of a million years. Malebo called from the bank, gesturing with his rifle. "Your turn to keep watch!" I dressed hurriedly and took the gun from him, training it along the grassy sand bank, wondering if I would have to shoot my first crocodile. Meanwhile, he walked into the current without removing a stitch of his uniform. Vicious Boy cheered him on.

Palm orchards—odors of unwashed working skin—shade— We had reached Stanley Pool, the impressive lake that presages the iron-black opacity of the interior upstream. An island dominates the center of the pool, M'Bamou, like a disc of shattered glass encircled by sharp fragments. Lear, Gloucester and the Fool—we investigated the loosely marshaled streets of Léopoldville, set out like a plantation district with the Company flag whipping on its mast above us, upon a tor of rippling grass. Large parasol trees shadowed the dusty avenues as the sun bled out on the swollen horizon. Uniformed men drifted between sullen knots of slaves. The cargo was taken care of and I left Malebo and the boy playing checkers on the gloomy veranda of our hut.

Through rush-fenced streets, I found my way to the office of the General Manager, where I was to present myself.

The man lived in a squalid mud building with a lean-to of brittle thatch propped against it. This appeared to have been part of a porch structure that had collapsed quite recently. There were two men inside the hut. The interior was illuminated with petroleum lamps. No sooner had I crossed the threshold, I was stunned by the noxious reek of vomit. The General Manager, the shorter of the two men, stood behind his desk, gripping its edges, leaning slightly forward, and regurgitating a yellow-gray broth of bile and hippopotamus fats into a silver ice bucket. The other man, an agent with a split pronged beard, stood close to him, impassively turning the pages of a small notebook by lifting the edges of the leaves with the tip of his pencil. Neither of them registered my presence for some moments. Instead, while the stocky manager bellowed into his bucket, the agent continued to recite some report. He spoke in an abbreviated code, punctuated by numbers and volumes and schedules that he evidently regarded as unimpressive from his flat tone of voice. I spoke up, introducing myself, startling both men.

"Ah! So, you're the New Dead Man," the General Manager smiled, a slight froth of stomach acid at the corners of his mouth. The agent did not immediately offer any such delicate opinion. "We've been impatient for you, haven't we, Émile?"

"How do you do, Sir?" The agent eyed me from toenail to scalp, tentatively extending his hand. It seemed that he suspected in me something novel and untrustworthy.

The General Manager introduced himself as Montagu. He wiped his face with a pristine white towel. "I'm quite all right," he said. "Not ill. Nothing contagious. You see, I put my fingers down my throat, and I clean myself out. It's almost religious with me, isn't it, Émile? But, my intestines are as clean as a chapel font." He clapped his hands together and a fat Negro boy shambled in, wordlessly retrieving the stinking bucket. The boy brushed past me on his way out, sloshing. I watched the General Manager drain a bottle of quinine tonic in one draw. I could feel the bearded agent staring at me. "The man we had inside has been dead for more than six weeks. The bloody forest will be glutted with wasting ivory, walking about still attached to those ugly gray faces. Émile, here, was set on becoming the replacement, but he has so very kindly deferred to my desire that he remain here in Léopoldville a little bit longer." The manager smirked at the agent. "And so, here you are! This is most fortunate, because Émile's my Holy Ghost. He sees what I cannot, and hears what I am not close enough to cop."—*And ignorant of his birth and parentage, became a bricklayer when he came of age*—

The ghost hung his head, flushing with shame. Émile, then, was a spy among the agents of the Central Station. I told Montagu that it might have been better for him not to disclose these matters so quickly if Émile was to do his work on me. And what of this dead man, whose station I was getting?

"A six-month'r. That's how long he survived in there before he blew his own brains out with a Company carbine. The Congo is filthy with six-month'rs, three-month'rs, and the odd nine-month'r. It's an attritional atmosphere in there. Both shade and sunlight bring you down, and the maddening isolation, also. How long do you give yourself, eh?" Montagu was blunt, in the way that cowards are. It was a cover for his pettifogging. He lathered his face and began to shave over a white basin. "Don't mind me. I'm here because I'm mediocre, but at least I know it, unlike some gentlemen I might name." The razor and his blue eyes flashed toward his spy. "Middle-aged, middle-distance, middle rank, middle-minded . . . That's why I need an ally, like young Émile here."

I said, "I don't intend to return."

The mediocre man laughed directly into my face, the bile on his breath like a fog of acid.

The agent did not laugh, though. "Come on, Kurtz," he offered, "I'll show you the sights."

The evening was sultry. Stepping outside of the mud hut, I saw from our elevation the lamp lit expanse of Léopoldville, strings of electric light bulbs swaying over the avenues and clustered buildings. We roamed districts where soldiers barracked, and awful shanties of broken slaves. There was a cimetiére full of plain crosses and utilitarian headstones, and there was a whitewashed church under red shingles. Inside it, someone was attempting to play a piano that had been warped by the climate. Then, I heard white men singing—*Mais voici du matin le lever radieux; Les ombres de la nuit seffacent dans les cieux; Tout danger est passé; notre course est finie. Gloire et louange soient à Dieu qui la bénie*—In a palm-draped alleyway, men in tawdry uniforms flickered like phantoms with shadowy black women, their naked breasts swaying rhythmically to the eerie music, as these couples collapsed to the ground, a monochrome of languid limbs and a strange sobbing—*The shadows of the night disappear into the heavens—All danger is passed; our race is over—*

*My effigy is more terrible than Christ—pallid and slaughtering ghost that I become—sorrowing tremens—*The following day, I went with Émile to Kinshasa, a primordial settlement a short distance along the south bank of Stanley Pool, inexorably eclipsed by Léopoldville, even as custom oscillated between the two. On the way to Kinshasa, I questioned Émile about my predecessor at the station, and his suicide by gunshot. The dead agent's name was Harold Carter, and everyone—that is Émile, Montagu, and possibly Janssens the Governor General and Severijns the phrenologist—had expected him to last, to "stick it out," as Émile expressed it. Had there been indications of his condition? "What might have emerged as a warning in a 'civilized' society, one simply ceases to register, in there," he said. There is an everyday madness in the Congo, a rippling plateau of insanity.

"Have you ever been inside a madhouse, Kurtz?"

"No. Never."

"Well, if you watch the inmates for long enough, it's the doctors who look touched."

"Did you intercept any correspondence from Carter?"

"Of course." Émile wiped his brow with his wrist.

"And?"

"Like any other white man: raging against the climate, the niggers, the isolation and the flies—always about his own limitless fortitude measured against the limitless lassitude of all others, and how a lesser man would go mad, etcetera, etcetera . . ."

"Did he have any family?"

"Yes, indeed, a large family, at that."

"They'll never receive the body, I imagine."

"The body, perhaps, but not the head."

We walked on, abstractedly watching the gray buzzards peeling from high branches. It was some minutes before we spoke again. I tried to imagine Harold Carter's family, a harsh monochrome image with the father sitting beside his wife, surrounded by hollow-eyed children. Had the news reached them, yet?

"Did you ever suspect murder?" I asked.

Émile didn't answer me. He licked his lips—his silence was a resonant affirmation blasting through the air over

Stanley Pool. He did suspect it, but never pressed his theory with Montagu. Carter's murder was understandable, reasoned from a cannibal perspective, or one of enslaved fury. Yet, if Montagu knew it, raising his head in slow recognition from his silver bucket of bile, then the reprisals would have been unthinkable, at least in the conscience of the Company spy—a hundred eyes for an eye.

Montagu, as I had witnessed on my arrival, was taking things at the station badly enough, as it was. His purging was an excuse for the symptoms of his panic, as deaths relayed up and down the river. There was nothing he could do about it. All that remained for Montagu was to wait.

The man who pulled the shotgun trigger, exploding Carter's brains all over the jungle, was almost certainly still there, waiting for me at the station. I wanted to know what Émile thought of this.

"I never said he was murdered."

Was Émile's absence of guile deliberate—his way of warning me?

"But," he continued, "many of his Negroes took the opportunity to emancipate themselves as he lay bleeding. Not all of them, but many."

"Did Carter write a suicide note, for his wife, to Montagu, or . . . to you?"

Émile shook his head. He lit a cigarette at the third attempt.

The satanic aspect of Kinshasa, I had not anticipated. It was early evening, under a bloated crimson sun. With Émile as my Virgil, I walked the inhospitable streets. Fires burned in empty metal cartridge boxes, and drums boomed from decaying buildings of mud and reclaimed European trash. Rats rolled in the sweltering gutters, running over our boots. I thought of Bruegel and plagues, darkening. Roosters clattered on a metal roof made from the flat hull of a sunken paddleboat. The red light that bathed Kinshasa menaced us through smoky alleys and streets defined by troughs of dry earth. Skinned and unrecognizable animals were draped on the clay walls, swarmed over by green-black flies. Pot bellied children hobbled naked through the dust, sucking on biscuits discarded by Company agents. Oil colored women swaggered in the acrid clouds of ash and the smoke of some creature scorching over a pyre at the corner of what Émile described as an important street. It was hard to see. They moved like undulating serpent-women, naked as Medusa, adorned with savage jewelry. The men shifted around us, brooding like prisoners watching their jailors making their rounds. "They know the consequences," Émile whispered. "We're perfectly safe." Still, I saw that his hand was on the butt of his revolver, to drive the point home.

When we came to the place Émile had been looking for, there was a crowd of Negroes already assembled, surrounding a square marked out with four burning torches. The warm air warped about us, disturbed by a prurient expectation. "I can smell the blood here, from before. Can you?" He was right. In every particle of earth carried on the cooling night breeze, I caught the rusting iron fumes of it, turning rotten. A new drumming began, low and guttural, as the glottal boast of some invisible monster. Boom. Boom. "Here she comes: the ndoki." I asked Émile, did he mean a witch? He smiled, betraying the faintest trace of nervousness. I watched, amazed, as she came through the dark mob. They parted for her, a shriveled woman dressed in a textile that resembled black wool. A fist turned in my stomach, wrapping its fingers around my spinal column. In each of her claws, the witch held a flapping rooster upside down, by its legs. The crowd closed in behind her, and she stood holding the wild birds in the center of the flaming square. It was only then that I saw that she was wearing a blindfold of the same black wool. She passed one bird toward the other, so that she held both roosters in one skinny hand, dangling and quarreling viciously. As her fingers shifted along their bony legs, it was impossible to separate them in the twists of ringlet-circled skin. A small boy, perhaps approaching the beginnings of puberty, stepped forward before her, and gave her a fifth burning torch. She held herself erect, pointing at us with the flames, embers spitting upwards into the gloom. I clutched at my notebook and tried to sketch what I saw. The drumming increased, frenzied and deafening. When it stopped, the witch released her basilisks and the two birds tore at each other. This cockfight could not have lasted long, but it occurs to me now as hideously drawn out—cracked wings, raking talons and hammering beaks tangling on the foul earth, eyeless sockets trickling red. The crowd of Negroes howled for it, hollering with rooster calls and punching the air in front of them. It was grotesque. The dead bird and the almost dead bird were taken away and finished off with a yank of the neck. It was time for the main event. The witch returned to consecrate the bloody ground. And what I witnessed then, I shall never forget. "Here we are." Émile pointed across the improvised ring to a big youth in the far corner.

He was magnificent, an animate idol of obsidian, shining in the embers of the sun and the staked corners of fire. The big youth was the Minotaur leaving his labyrinth, his beautiful eyes turned toward the sky, apprehending the approach of a new moon. His hair was a close fuzz of jet black, his brow high and dignified. Between the brown blades of his cheeks, his wide nostrils flared, as the witch smeared the air with burning herbs. For a moment, I saw him wreathed in purple smoke. He took one imperious pace forward, poised and impassive in front of the ragged crowd that penned him inside the ring. His opponent was in front of us. This other bore the scars of the chicotte in layers of raised crosses across his back. He raised his raw fist into the night and an ululating cry went up with it. The woman in black wool rolled her purple smoke over his shoulders. This other, closer to us, glimmered in the flickering orange light. He was muscular, supple, his head lolling on his neck. Émile told me that he had seen this one before. From our left, a Company agent broke through the boundary of flesh, clapping his hands and blowing a silver whistle. All fell silent. The witch retreated, and the drumming, which I had almost ceased to notice since it had become inseparable from the percussion of my heart and chasing blood, stopped.

There was no boxing bell, so the Company agent blew his shrill whistle once and gestured for each of the Negroes to advance into the fight. Both held their fists up in the proper way and maneuvered, their trunks rotating, their elbows held in. "I told you," Émile enthused. "The cocks are horrible savages, but these men are like true English boxers." The agent pulled out a pocket watch on a chain, almost as an afterthought. The boxers stalked one another, flicking out jabs that were met with disciplined blocks, forearms and swiveling bodies. A cloud of dust rose about their ankles. At first, the match was observed in almost silent expectation. Clanking and metallic dragging let the spectators know that the boxers were in shackles. Émile said that the chains helped maintain a disciplined boxing stance. The first round was cagey and quite uneventful, except for when the one with the scars who had been nearest us got off a nasty rabbit punch after the big youth had seemed to duck under him. The agent let out a litany of obscenities, but the bout continued. When the whistle sounded and each man returned to his torch-lit corner, there was a restrained, disappointed murmuring. Émile remarked that it was usually this way, no matter who was fighting, until the third or fourth round whistle. The Company agent was called Smythe, an unremarkable man except that he arbitrated these boxing matches. Between the rounds, each of the crow-black men drank palm wine from a seashell, while the nonchalant Smythe studied his timepiece. The whistle sounded again. The boxer with the scarred back, who had been to us for all of the fight so far, rushed out, performing a series of cartwheels in his chains, screaming madly. The witch in her blindfold emitted a jackal cry, throwing up violet fog and a strip of gunpowder sunbaked into a zebra hair whip, crackling fireworks exploding all about her. The firecrackers and the spell confused the big youth, just long enough for his antagonist to circle behind him and to leap up upon his back. If it is possible for a man to grin as he sinks his teeth deep into the flesh of another man's neck, I saw it in those terrible white teeth that flashed in the flames. Above the din, Émile shouted into my ear. "So much for your Marquis of Queensbury!" It was Vicious Boy, hanging like a vampire with his arms wrapped around the big youth's throat! I saw how foolish I had been, imagining—on the long march from Matadi—that I had seen some traces of innocence in him. The boy was as cruel as anything in Nature.

"Smythe must stop this!" I protested.

"He won't," said Émile.

I watched Smythe, the whistle lifted close to his lips, but never to them.

"He can't . . ."

The big youth threw Vicious Boy from his back and stood upon his ankle chains so that he could not kick. He thrust his knees down into the boy's ribs, shattering them.

Blood erupted from between Vicious Boy's teeth. The big youth back-haired him and dragged him upright. Vicious Boy resisted, flailing and crying, his fingernails scratching into the other's eyes. But he was expiring beneath a deluge of black-fisted blows. The larger Negro tried to hold Vicious Boy to his feet while he beat him, but he slipped out of his grip and slumped to the red earth. I saw a white rib projecting from Vicious Boy's skin, a gray sac of ripped lung with it. Something gruesome bubbled from his gaping mouth, between the brilliant distorted teeth. His eyes were blank. Smythe stood stunned at the center of the ring. The big youth stood panting over the diminishing brown corpse. Émile said nothing. The witch stepped out of the crowd, slowly unwinding her blindfold. When she saw Vicious Boy mutilated below her, she began sobbing. Something drew me forward—magnetism. Smythe was shaking on his spot. His silver whistle lay in the dirt. I stood in the ring, extending my hand to the big youth, convinced of him, as one is convinced by the reemergence of a dream in daylight.

Nsumbu has been with me ever since.

*A sacrificial chamber—parasol brides splash London walls with their scarlet wealth—death loves the footlights—mica in the clotted mud—*The return to Léopoldville that night was made in silence, the two us probing for the right words, and these remaining elusive—phantasmal emotions slipping effortlessly through the over-examined bone of my skull. Nsumbu walked between us, shivering from the residue of violence. We were almost back to the fenced in streets when Émile's dry voice startled me.

"Some of his effects are in your quarters."
"Whose effects?"
"Harold Carter's things . . ."
I hadn't noticed. The place was disordered so that, at first,

nothing projected incongruously. I had taken the hash of objects to be the various discards of other expeditions that had stopped at the station, and I thought better of taking them further in. Now, some of the objects imprinted themselves luminously upon me: the half-consumed gin bottle, the red paisley smoking jacket, the strange ebony fetish reminiscent of the Venus of Willendorf, the shotgun on the wall, breached at a right angle, its walnut stock traced with talcum and iodine, the oil paints on the window sill, and the easel propped in the corner in a pile of civilian clothes, like a spear impaling a sunken corpse. Émile had examined the gun for fingerprints. It occurred to me that I would be in that room for two more nights, more if there were a delay with my boat. The room was haunted, by Harold Carter, by Vicious Boy, and by the encroaching of the evil outside. And the boat would be delayed by some poltergeist in the boiler as they constructed it on the bank of the Pool.

"It's funny. Macabre, really. We did retrieve Carter's body. We even got it down to Matadi, to load it aboard a steamboat to Boma. The dockworkers refused to unload it, and it came back, only to go out again. Backwards and forwards went Harold Carter's headless corpse in its stupid coffin. The niggers must have known that it was a crime. There was a taboo on it. Eventually, Rommel took it off and burned it."

Émile and I sat upon the hill overlooking Léopoldville, the tall flagpole at our back, the starry blue colors slapping like a sail. We watched the lights on those brittle Belgian streets going out. Soon, we were in the darkness of a kind of Calvary. It seemed appropriate, since I had first encountered him beside the corpses and quicklime of an open grave, that I gathered Vicious Boy's burial went unmarked. I never knew his real name. I could have asked, but it seemed pointless. I had demanded that Smythe remove the shackles from Nsumbu's ankles and I had taken him to recover in the crude quarters I shared with Malebo, the half-caste. Malebo did not weep for Vicious Boy. I'm not certain if I had expected him to mourn or not. Malebo dressed the vivid bite wound on Nsumbu's neck and treated the scratches and abrasions on his face. The big youth exhibited signs of shock. He shivered and stared blandly toward the white cloth flapping at the window. I took off my jacket and wrapped it around his shoulders, careful not to aggravate his pains. On the hill, drinking a harsh red wine with Émile, it was not difficult to imagine that we were the only wakeful men for a hundred miles. The garbage glow of Kinshasa paled and died. In the moonlight, I found that Émile was staring at me. He seemed quite unlike a spy, then.

"Do you hate this place, yet?" he asked. "Perhaps not hate, exactly, but I wonder if you feel that creeping scorn that comes to Company men, even if they don't have it when they arrive."

"I like it." I meant what I said.

On Émile's thin, bearded face, there was a strange, admiring smile.

I tried to look over the benighted wilderness, thinking of another man's words—*'Tis an unweeded garden that grows to seed; things rank and gross in nature possess it merely*—A curtain of obsolescence draped over the town. I told him: "The Company's grip on these places is slipping already."

"Montagu wouldn't believe you," Émile said, "nor Jans-sens and their cronies. I'm no crony, Kurtz. I've seen some-thing of what you mean, but what about it? They brought you here, and if the Company were to fall back—"

"They are injecting me into the heart. The Company is merely the needle. So *merely* the needle . . ."

She is Nsumbu's wife, I think. Last night, she found me crawling toward the Pit, intercepting me on the way to see my ivory. Her long fingernails ripped my neck as she rutted against me, this feral queen the shade of tamarind. Her belly was swollen against me.

*Yellala falla—the bullish water between the crags, growling— black kites—*After four days, our steamer had been made ready, its paddle blades stripped of lurid algae with wire brushes. Tendrils of vegetation had spiraled behind us as we rounded Kinshasa. In the daylight, the yellow beach, slopes of shale, and the quiet brown jetties suggested nothing of the night before. It might have been a stretch of Brighton, before the terraces and the seaside tat bulged from the land toward the tideline in a gaudy limestone wave. The three of us, Malebo, Nsumbu and I, barely left the room. I didn't tell them that the odd miscellany of abandoned gear in the place had belonged to Harold Carter. Malebo finished the gin, and Nsumbu rolled up the flamboyant satin smoking jacket for use as a pillow. He slept on the floor, in the spectral outline where Vicious Boy had made his bed, and he wore my Company jacket, even while he slept. He and Malebo exchanged no words while we waited, but seemed to negotiate one another well enough. It was the first time that I had worked with oil paints since Broadmoor.

But, I was wrong about Johnny Malebo's grief. It was there, submerged. It burst out of him as we navigated Dover Cliffs, out of Stanley Pool. It was a monstrous bark of pain that ricocheted along the white ravine cut by the river. I happened to be standing ahead of him on the deck, scanning the lugubrious water for hippos with what had been Harold

Carter's shotgun. Instinctively, I whipped about and raised the weapon at the epicenter of that unspeakable cry, only to find my sights on the half-caste—his mouth still gaping, white fronds of saliva connecting his teeth, his eyes rolled back in that vaguely colored face. He was drenched in sweat, his hands clawed in front of his chest. Yet, as suddenly as it surfaced, it was gone, racing ahead of us along the pallid cliff walls, and Malebo began to breathe again, in possession of his soul. As I lowered the rifle, his hands returned slowly to his sides, and then into his pockets. He remained that way for a moment, suffused in a silver mist of guilt. Staring at the deck between my boots, he inhaled deeply, letting his eyes apprehend me inch by inch, until our gazes met. He whispered, "I'm sorry, Kurtz. I didn't know it was there." Again, I thought of Montagu, emptying himself into his silver ice bucket. And I thought: Grief, too, is an unhygienic thing.

Beyond those Dover Cliffs, I stared into the ambiguous plexus of the jungle, my eyes skimming stones across the surface of the wash until the unending film of green water and the overhanging slither of the boughs became one vortex of emerald light. This vivid barrel may have been the last image that Harold Carter ever saw. We were travelling inside a serpentine shaft of air in a choking forest. It was the sluggish vertigo of the end of time, when the clocks are outrun and man stands aghast with all the stars behind him, his fingers still outstretched, feeling for the black limits of his life. It was an opium dream—languid gorillas in the long grass—golden serpents dripping from the trees. Moving in the final fathoms toward it, what would I find at my station, smoldering beams and scorched earth, three dozen shackled and starving Negroes ransacking all the food inside the perimeter? Would any of them have remained there, after the station chief's death?

*Gargantuan baobab trees—hollow skulls in antlers—coral necklace—*The captain of our last steamer was an Irishman named Devlin, and he wore the shirt and collar of priest as he manned the wheel, sweating profusely in the pilothouse. His skin was closely freckled, even his scalp where he had shaved his head. His fingers were stained with engine grease, and this blackened the sockets around his green eyes as he struggled to keep the sweat from settling in pools there. His cadaverous head nearly touched the wooden parapet that kept him in shade. I stood with him as he piloted us between the sand bars that were almost invisible beneath the flashing current. Devlin was familiar and canny with all the subtle shifts in the surface, and expert enough to converse with me, even while ostensibly he was deep in concentration at his steering. This missionary sailor had been Carter's assistant, he revealed. He had not been back since the agent's death. But, he had himself urged the cannibals to wait there for a new station chief. I was not surprised to discover that he knew and had worked closely with Carter. Despite its immense span, and the hunger of empire, there were relatively few whites in the bush. It was natural that they would overlap, and form a chain of nervous acquaintance, watching one another for signs of degeneration, counting their days. For Devlin, delivering me to the station was to be his final act upon the Congo. The missionary fever that had brought him there had broken at last, and all of his delusions with it. He would wear his stained white collar and black shirt only as far as his return to a freighter at Banana. After that port, he would hurl his priest's uniform into the Atlantic, where no man knew him. That he wore it still was only a concession to avoid explaining its absence to Montagu and his kind. I had to ask him what he made of Carter's death. His only response on this subject was: "What does it matter to me, now?" He was desperate to be a stranger on the sea. Taking a glass of whisky, I went down and reposed in the steamer's blunt bow, my white shirt almost transparent, and there like an angel I slept . . .

In the Palm Pavilion, I was beneath a great dome of intricately leaded glass, and the anesthetic was beginning to wear off. Tropics of blue ink sectioned the pale skin of my abdomen, more bulbous with fats than I remembered it. The sweetness of the chloroform scalded my throat and stripped the moisture from my nasal passages—fishhooks seeking a pharaoh's brain. The hot, rubber sealed cupola let in the sky, and in that cathedral, that pleasure dome of artificial flowers, lifeless ornaments, and marble statuary, I became aware of Thiriar's hands inside me, the good doctor's scalpels, pliers and fingers lost in the labyrinth of my gore. Open to the clouds on a bloodstained table, pecked at as Prometheus, bedeviled as Faust, stabbed as Hamlet, I was as noble as a pinned butterfly. Though Doctor Thiriar scraped in vain at the sponge of my cancer, I was yet the King. Leopold's body was too large for me. Our eyes misaligned as I slipped in and out of consciousness, so that my view out of his flesh was obstructed by bone and slimy strips of muscle. Locking my teeth into his jaw, I worked at his mouth, operating it, a Venus flytrap of claret and receding gums. Another cloth of chloroform dulled the sensation of cutting within my intestines. Thiriar appeared dejected. The tight curls of his beard collected his sweat as he withdrew from the work. His eyebrows conspired toward a singular expression of hagridden failure. I tried to mouth—*It doesn't matter, Jules*—but lack of motor control prevented it. The sheath of a fat king is difficult to manipulate when one is anesthetized. There were tears in the doctor's eyes as he knitted my skin back together with catgut stitches. I knew that the numbing would soon recede once and for all, and the pain would come roaring back to fill the silent spaces in my nerves. As soon as the agony of the surgery entered my guts, a young whore entered the Palm Pavilion to gaze upon my gray, wrinkled form. Severijns followed the girl, fluttering about her with his calipers and tape measure, making futile gestures toward examining her skull for symptoms of syphilis and degeneracy, of which there might have been many, could he only apprehend her. The girl's brown hair was pinned up, and she wore a glimmering dress of gold, yellow and amber. With her flagrant lips and ivory complexion, the coolness of her bearing, she loitered upon the edge of the modern, and in my bedroom she was the cry of the future. From the incalculable distance of my delirium, I signed papers, fighting to operate the King's moribund hands while I lay imposed inside his evaporating marrow and desiccating bones. The whore began to weep. *How old fashioned,* I thought, *to mistake the mortality of monarchs.* Eventually, the bloody hollows of Leopold ceased to respond, and I lay trapped in his dead weight. The light of the greenhouse diffused, and the tuberose and false orchids wilted as I passed them. They ferried me out from under the dome and set me upon an ornate funeral litter, draped with valences of black, and plumed with dyed feathers and painted ferns. The awful scent of death rushed through the faints of chloroform, brushing aside the last barricades of life. The body of Leopold hardened. The funeral cortege wove through the arcades of Laeken, and south toward the Royal Palace and the center of Brussels, flocked over with soldiers and cardinals led by gaunt and mitered Mercier with his golden crucifix. I was carried before the Palace in a haze of rain, misting on the uneven stones. The white-bearded head lolled stiffly to the left, and I stared out from the sockets of his eyes, shifting within the corpse for a better view—sudden sound of breaking glass. All of the windows of the Royal Palace exploded outwards, showering the cortege in a storm of starry shards. It was as if every room and every corridor had been packed with dynamite, and the fuses had smoldered until my arrival. The eight men who bore me dropped the litter, and a loose tooth fell into my throat. As I looked, thousands of Negroes leaned and pressed through the smashed panes. Ominous, daubed for war, they ululated and drummed, spilling like serpents from the pale masonry, an overflowing tide of flesh, splitting out through the roof slates and curling the lead from the gutters. The elderly soldiers in the cortege grasped at their ceremonial swords. Yet, before any of those brightly polished blades could be drawn, hundreds of spears were thrown from the writing knots of cannibal warriors, breaking from the Palace like oil through coral. Immediately, the sky blackened with missiles. Men fell screaming all about me, trembling shafts penetrating them and clattering against the cobblestones. Choirboys were impaled against their masters. Wounded horses reared and fell in tangles of meat. The death scream of the funeral procession melted into the rasp of rainwater. The savages in the Palace sang and thumped their weapons against oval shields of antelope hide. I saw that the spears had torn through the black canopy of the litter above me. A dozen of these javelins projected from Leopold's corpse. The weight was suffocating, but the flesh was as insensate as a clot of clay. Then, a hundred Negro children poured from the Palace, surrounding the body, beating it with the cauterized stumps where their little hands had been. A terrible lamentation went up, but their faces did not change. I realized that the mourning was not for the King and his bastard colonies. It was for something deeper, and the mourning was mine.

Oui, j'ai les yeux fermés à votre lumière. Je suis une bête, un nègre. Mais je puis être sauvé. Vous êtes de faux nègres, vous maniaques, féroces, avares. Marchand, tu es nègre; magistrat, tu es nègre; général, tu es nègre; empereur, vieille démangeaison, tu es nègre: tu as bu d'une liqueur non taxée, de la fabrique de Satan.—Ce peuple est inspiré par la fièvre et le cancer.

"Monsieurs! S'il vous plait arrêter!" I was awakened by Johnny Malebo kicking the heel of my boot, and by a hollering from the starboard bank of the river. "Patienter, Monsieurs." The sun came in flyblown pillars of luminescence through the serrated canopy over the water, and I struggled to rouse myself, as if the suffocating weight of the dream was still upon me. I knuckled my eyes and searched the tree line for the man who was calling for us to stop and assist him. The half-caste pointed to a small promontory where several trees had been cleared. There, standing on a stump, close to an orderly pile of firewood, was a ragged figure. Devlin sounded the steamer's whistle in acknowledgment, and we turned toward the marshy bank, cautious of snags in the brown weeds. "Merci, merci," the figure crooned. His accent was neither French, nor Belgian, but faintly Slavic. As we drew closer, I heard Devlin muttering, "What in God's name . . . ?" When we were near enough to the bank, I leapt ashore. "Bonjour!" The man saluted me, rather informally, and I glanced back over my shoulder to where Nsumbu stood on the deck wearing my Force Publique jacket.

"Who are you?" I asked him, extending my hand like a white man.

"I am Nikolai Junker, of the Van Shuyten Expedition—formerly ship's doctor out of Petersburg—formerly amateur physician in Moscow—formerly nobody in Tambov—now to be, hopefully, your sputnik." He wore a red rag in his thin blonde hair, and his beard was unevenly cut, as though he had hacked at it with a blunt knife.

"Where is the rest of your expedition?"

Indifferently, he raised his shoulders. His clothes had been repaired so many times, that it was difficult to tell the original fabric from the patches. Perhaps it was once khaki, or brown, I could not say.

"Who is Van Shuyten? Is he with you, somewhere?"

"No, he's at—what's it called? Sonho, at the estuary, or I suppose that he is—Dutchman—Big slaver, and successful seller of dry goods. He had his rifle butt upholstered with leopard skin. He was my patron."

Behind him was a grass hut in the shadow of a Russian navy flag, the white, blue, and red frayed and tattered. Pieces of it had been absorbed into the man's strange costume. Evidently, he had improvised this small firewood station in the wetlands, and recently, because Devlin had not seemed to know it.

"You're here alone?" I looked at the detritus that spilled form his hovel of reeds.

"Yes," he said reflectively, "I am quite alone. I have been for . . . months."

He seemed so radically deracinated that, by the odds, he should have been dead. Certainly, he smelled like an evicted corpse. If he had survived in there for that long, then he had not done so in the manner of any other colonist I had seen. He disappeared into his hut, closing the red curtain that sufficed as his door behind him. I followed, battling the heaves of nausea that the stink of his place forced upon me. On an uneven table of his construction, an appalling cloud of insects fed on a lump of crocodile meat. The Russian hastily gathered his scant possessions: a packet of tobacco, a revolver, and a decaying book that he tucked into the waist of his trousers. He smiled, expectantly. I told him that I could not allow him to come aboard our steamer if he did not bathe beforehand. Reluctantly, he placed his things back on the table, beside the foul carrion. Outside, I watched him walk into the river, unbuttoning his shirt. He submerged repeatedly, a yellowish scum encircling him as he performed his ablutions. Malebo, Devlin and Nsumbu all observed, fascinated and slightly disgusted. Our missionary pilot threw the Russian a bar of Pears' soap. As he undressed, his clothes floated about him, and finally with the soap a white lather replaced the filth. Retreating into the hovel once more, I retrieved his things for him, and waited on the bank. Naked in the water, scrubbing dutifully at his clothes, his shoulders reddening in the sun, the Russian kept his eyes on his book, which I held in my left hand, the revolver in my right. It was an antiquarian volume of British navigation tables, annotated with his own Cyrillic scrawl in the margins. Something irrational informed me that this was his secret report on the ill-starred expedition, and that, in time, my own name might appear as a pencil note there, also. Just as Émile was retained by the Company to spy on the other agents, so all of the whites of the Congo had taken to snide modes of gossip and subtle espionage. When all was said and done, they were as jealous siblings hanging on the words of a will and testament that did not include them. I raised my eyes again from the stained pages to the blonde man in the drink.

"Did you ever meet a station manager named Carter?" I asked.

He had not.

I was disappointed. "Or Montagu?"

Again, the answer was negative.

I continued to thumb through the volume, and the Russian watched me as he dressed in the water and waded slowly to the bank. Then, he was before me, dripping on the grass, snatching the book from my hand, snarling "Spasibo." Just as he took it from me, and with a jolt that I was compelled to conceal from him, I noticed a word in English, a name: Harry. The Russian was lying. The chains of a mysterious heredity ran through the channels of the country, where each man watched his own back. The Company leant a weak dignity to this mercenary coup. Johnny Malebo extended a plank for us, and Nikolai Junker and I boarded the steamer, its paddles slapping the green current.

Sitting astern, I listened to more of the Russian's story. We drank coffee from tin cups, and he cleaned and oiled his revolver with some of my supplies. Junker explained that his own steamer had struck a reef, had been breached and sank between Banana and Boma. Malebo enthusiastically confirmed this wreck, except he said that particular boat had gone down in the channel two years ago. At this, the passenger in his stitched rags stared at the half-caste in disbelief. Turning his gaze to the rotating machinery behind us, the iridescent splashing and the widening wake, his voice was little more than a whisper: "It could not have been so long . . ." *No,* I thought, *perhaps it had not been.* After describing his deceased father as an archpriest of the orthodox Dalmatian tradition at the Transfiguration Cathedral, Junker purloined shaving soap and a blade from Devlin. When he was finished with it, his aspect was inexplicably youthful. He had told us already that he was twenty-three, but he did not appear a minute over seventeen, his small blue eyes shifting like a schoolboy's under interrogation—a guilty thing under the blind stripes of the jungle. How was it possible that this Junker had been alone in there for as long as he claimed, traipsing along the river territory, like an orphan, without encountering another party? Had he been at Harold Carter's station? I did not tell him that the same place was our destination, nor, at first, that I was the new manager.

*Iridescent water—the languid verandah of Caliban in his uniform—chewing a plagued head—*At nightfall, the anchor was kedged and the steamer settled in the channel, swaying subtly in the viridescent flow. It was an oppressive Nubian sky that closed in upon us, almost tangibly pressing Malebo, Nsumbu and I into a corner at the stern of the boat, where we lit wax candles, conjuring our shrinking amber cove against the darkness. Devlin slipped limply from the helm and into the succor of a lapsed religious sleep. Nikolai Junker in his colorful swatches collapsed exhausted between two tea chests of supplies. In the diminishing arc of our light, in a more civilized setting, we might have told ghost stories over our coffee and claret. Yet, this artery was a phantasmagoria all its own.

The eyes of the other two men glistened—Malebo's mismatched along the fault of his race—and the African's now recalling lead shot in melting snow. Nsumbu, I discovered that night, knew some rudimentary English. Malebo and I were quite astonished with the primitive sound of it, and whence he learned it. A fractured conversation was possible between us, and from my intuition of some of the vocabulary and gestures of the half-caste and the Negro—I even gleaned some of the old language of the Congo. It was rudimentary, as the first utterances of any foreign tongue will be, and yet we managed, and were good company. Malebo, either diluted black, or diluted white, adjusted to Nsumbu's presence. He seemed to grasp that the savage boy that Nsumbu had overthrown had it coming to him.

Vicious Boy had been a beast in regalia, and never would have been anything else. Nsumbu was easier. I gave him a cigarette. In stuttering coils of language and smoke, we located the past.

Somewhere, beyond the veil, was the station where Harold Carter had died and where this curious trinity of ours would live. Nsumbu confessed that he was familiar with the place, and with Carter. It was from that station that he had absconded, only to be captured outside of Kinshasa and inducted into the remotest schemes of the Marquis of Queensbury, boxing in a fire lit slum. Nsumbu had been in Kinshasa for six months. Therefore, he could say nothing about the fatal bullet. It meant little that he broke free of Carter's station. He would have worked to escape any of the Company's outposts. He remembered the dead manager as a bland creature, not overly cruel, nor unusually sympathetic. His hauls of ivory—*dínu ya nzawu*—were unexceptional, and under a ragged arc of bats, Nsumbu spoke obliquely of a rival in the same Company uniform, dogging the station. And yet, he may have been talking merely of Carter's suspicions. It was impossible to say. Malebo shrugged and I gave Nsumbu another cigarette.

Of all the men I had encountered, even so fleetingly, since that day on the beach at Calais, this tar-skinned alien was the only one whose loyalty—camaraderie even—seemed important to me, and inexplicably so. That he might desire to escape my station inspired in me a disproportionate torment. It had not occurred to me that this might be what it is to possess another man as inconsequentially as one might own a set of Brussels porcelain. I resolved that it was better for him to be ignorant of the details of Carter's death. In my vanity, and the mystery of that claustrophobic night,

I thought perhaps that we might discover them together. The moon was a saucer of bone.

*Tuxedoes slipping into the drugged wilderness—lolling on the drunken delta—sketching water lilies and crying like babies—*He was strange, this Junker, something between a peacock and a plumed serpent. His movements were languid and yet his gestures were deliberate, calculated. As a boy, he had always been a truant and a runaway, he said, and I warmed to this aspect of the man, even as I was suspicious of him. Those first hours spent with him on the steamer, faltering and navigating the tangles of the anfractuous river through the claw-fisted conifers, were like peeling dead fingers from their treasure. The Russian was by turns furtive and gracious. I watched him, and listened as he boasted to Malebo, indicating the record of certain incredible events in the marginalia of his brittle copy of *An Inquiry into Some Points of Seamanship,* supposing that his squared-off hand-writing in a language that none of us could read was proof of his flukes and casual defiance of the jungle. He orated his frozen voyage out of Petersburg, cutting through an ice flow and blinding white waves. He spoke of his experiences later on Dutch and French vessels, performing an amputa-tion on a wounded sapper along the Ivory Coast. The words spilled like pennies from a torn pocket, and rang all around us in bewildering ellipses that could not quite be grasped. Yet, most of his itinerant career as a doctor of sorts involved merely the dispensing of laudanum to the frostbitten slums forgotten by the Tsar. Even Junker's father, the archpriest, had admired the Narodniks, the assassins with their bombs arrayed in the flour and cabbage leaves of their kitchen tables. The young Junker, the runaway was more ambivalent in his sympathies, still part of the mass of the impoverished that cannot resist the baubles of monarchy and the glamor of tyranny. "Oh, it's a bind. It's difficult for any man, and the Tsar is a man, in the end, not an angel. A Devil? I doubt it."

"Why are you here, Nikolai?" Johnny Malebo interrupted him.

"There's more for me than morphine and fishwives and bricklayers passed out in the snow. I quit a postal ship at the mouth of the river and made a nuisance of myself with the Dutch and the niggers back there. I thought that Van Shuyten's patronage was all fine luck. I convinced him and he kitted me out. Then the jinx, and my boat cracked like an egg on that reef. It went down as if it was hungry for the black mud beneath it, and men drowned in a circle of grease and froth." Nikolai Junker stared at his hands like Lady Macbeth. "I got ashore with a few scraps, whatever flotsam I could drag out . . ."

"Alone for two years," I said, studying his reconstructed uniform. "You must have seen a lot of dead men."

Junker regarded me, the sun in his eyes forcing him to squint. His lips tightened together. I fancy that, at that moment, he may have had an intuition about our heading, that he recognized this passage of the swell. He must have known also that it was too late for him to fabricate some pretext for leaving the boat. An ivory agitation bloomed through his face, setting his blue eyes in livid contrast.

"You've a way with words, Kurtz."

In turn, all of us were interrupted by the acrid scent of smoke. A delicate silver fog hung over the reach, this wraith enveloping the steamer in silence. Only the churn of the paddles echoed within it. Then I watched a menacing shape revolve out of the canopy, the aberrant column billowing through the twisted branches. We were close enough to the station for Devlin to surmise that the place was burning or had already burned to the ground. "It must be the station," he opined, disconsolately.

"Keep us moving, Devlin," I insisted. Was there to be nothing but cinders and ashes at the end of my journey? For as much as I resisted this anxiety, the distant rumble and cackle of a significant fire was unmistakable.

"What are you laughing at, bloody nigger?" Johnny Malebo shoved Nsumbu against the wooden bulkhead that wrapped around the boiler. But, the black youth's smile was fixed with profound satisfaction. "Cheshire Cat, bastard! I'll wipe that smile off." The half-caste struck him with an open palm across the face—the sound of a whip crack.

"Enough!" I pushed between them. "I'll brook no more of this, Malebo."

He was sullen, panting from the wash of his violence.

As we rounded the final sawtooth of fetid lagoons, we all saw the station. It was intact. Nsumbu touched his mouth and made a small gesture of fluttering fingers at me. This, I understood only much later, was his manner of informing me that he had sent word ahead that I was approaching.

A gang of Negroes worked like horticulturalists and land-scapers, reclaiming a space that had been desecrated and mostly abandoned. Beyond their dismal color and naked-ness, they might have been any other gardeners at Kew, or the Palm Pavilion . . .

"What are they burning?" I pointed at a pyre.

"Katolika . . ." Nsumbu said.

I had to restrain Devlin. "Bloody cannibals! Our mission-aries!"

"Ve!" Nsumbu shook his head, protesting vigorously, as Devlin tried to draw his revolver with trembling fingers, unable to open the fastener on his canvas holster.

"He's right, Devlin. No, it's a stack of Bibles. It's just a stack of Bibles."

"Sacrosanct," he complained. "What blasphemy is this, Nsumbu?"

"What does it matter to you, Devlin?" I demanded. I pushed his hands away from his belt, and opened his holster myself. "What do you call a man who deserts his post, but is yet too much a coward to cast off the uniform? Be a man, Devlin. I'll not let you hide behind piety to make your killing on your way out." Pulling out his gun, I threw it into the wake of the boat. Devlin stared at the rippling algae. I gripped his wet chin, turning his face about, like a dog in a starched clerical collar. "You want to kill a man over something you don't even believe in?" Letting my hand trail down his throat to his collar, I ripped the white fabric from its buttons. "As manager of this station, I forbid you to disembark. You'll stay on this blasted steamer until we're unloaded, and then directly you'll turn around. We'll give you firewood enough to get you back to Léopoldville at a fair rate of knots. You know the snags by heart, don't you? Don't dare to interfere with this station, or grass on me to Montagu, his spy, nor anyone else. I held the frayed clerical collar between my fingertips. In the sunlight through the smoke, it fluttered as the steamer thumped into the marsh. Devlin stared, transfixed upon the shreds of his hypocrisy, until I released the collar and it fluttered into the water and was taken away by the current. "You're a free man, now, Devlin." There were tears on his face. "Now," I said, "Shut up, stand down, then piss off."

*A gorilla ripping the masonry from the clock tower—ringing the great bell like Quasimodo—reflected in the opal panes of the clock face—*From the bank of the Congo where the bonfire snapped and flared, and smoldering leaves of paper twisted in the rising smoke, the bush land that flowed in a gradient away from the water had been cleared. A clean bite had been taken out of the undergrowth, so that there appeared to be a bright lawn, rising on the hillside away from the jetty. Several reed huts had been constructed on that lawn, and above all of these was the rectangular station building. Malebo, with Nsumbu still wearing the Company field jacket that I had never thought of taking back from him, organized working parties to unload my luggage and supplies, and to carry the few remaining tusks of ivory back to the steamboat.

I moved toward the station house, a somnambulist lost in a dream of a savage country where he is, as all dreamers will be, invincible. It was two hundred yards away from the channel, and those final footfalls were the strangest of the voyage. The noises of the station receded. From within my vacuum, I observed the Negroes mouthing words that never reached my ears, drums and heavy work that I never heard. I thought of Monsieur Prudhomme drifting dumbly to his gallows, dropping wordlessly through the trapdoor, where I saw his dead legs kicking. My heart beat hard in my breast as I climbed the sweat-backed rise. When I reached the door, set behind a flimsy screen, I could hear the blood booming in my arteries, and my rasping breath skinning my lungs. It was an ecstatic panic—like being born. When I pulled back the screen and touched the door, the jungle contracted. The sun was above the house.

Inside, it was the *Mary Celeste*. The interior had lain undisturbed since the death of the previous occupant. Sticky blue flies subsisted on the red residue of a glass of evaporated wine. Some of them buzzed weakly on the lacquered table beside the unmade bed. I poked about the desk, pulling open the drawers, feeling my sweat chill in the shaded room. There was no sign of any Company reports. Neither did I find any journals or correspondence more personal to the ghost. I wrenched the wooden crucifix from its nail above the bed. It felt like a weapon. If Harold Carter had committed suicide, was this totem the reason why he did it outside, close to the tree line? Was this wooden witness too accusatory? I walked with it down the hill to the bonfire. I cast it into the flames with the wrecked Bibles. There were about two-dozen Negroes at the station, as well as I could count, then. Malebo and Nsumbu stood between the pyre and the bizarre ziggurat of cargo unloaded from Devlin's boat. He had the vessel sputtering away from the jetty. I pointed to a pile of the half-immolated missionary books. Through the half-caste, I inquired: "Your idea, Company man?"

Nsumbu stiffened, suppressing the amusement he felt. "Mú. Éé!"

I replied: "Ya mbóté!" *Good.* The missionaries were an infestation. It was evident that my predecessor had not done enough to discourage them, bent under his own spiritual cowardice. It was one thing to take possession of the abundant materials of the place, but to insult their primordial souls—"Where's Junker?"

Malebo pointed to a grass hut half way between the river and my quarters. The Russian lay in the doorway, twitching like an animal in his dreams. That first night, I sought him out, inviting him to help me drink a bottle of good champagne.

Zebra killed with Martini-Henrys—holes in my furniture— Through the remains of the day, Nsumbu had been of excellent assistance to me. He dragged out Carter's bedding, stale with the phantom of his sweat, and worked with me to install my possessions in their proper places. There were photographs of Carter's wife left in silver frames. She was young and fair-haired. Her eyes had a piercing melancholy—a woman lost in fog. These and a few other remnants, a fountain pen, an embroidered handkerchief, an ivory comb with a clinging strand of hair, I kept in a

Huntley and Palmer's biscuit tin, giving the digestives to Nsumbu. I washed my face in an enamel basin, pitying the man who had carried the heavy bowl from Matadi. I shaved with a sandalwood lather and a new blade before changing my clothes. In the pewter mirror, my skin was darker. My ears and the bridge of my nose were red, and my brow freckled and tanned. I dressed in a pristine shirt of white linen that only exaggerated the work of the sun. For the lower half, I wore gray pajama trousers and felt like a poet. In spite of some flickering thoughts of poisonous spiders, ants and centipedes, I went barefoot. I lanced my blisters with a sewing needle that I sterilized with a match. I wanted the air to get at the sores. Junker rapped on the screen door at about eight, as I recall. I was still holding the sewing needle as the man of rags stepped into the light of my oil lamps. It glinted, and the coincidence relaxed him. We made small talk and began drinking the champagne. He said that he admired my porcelain. It did not take long for the alcohol to redden the rims of his blue eyes, and he kicked off his brogues, informing me that he had bought them from a Scotsman who had worn them peat digging, but that they drained beautifully. He had polished his shoes ahead of visiting me, yet wore no socks. The scarlet hems of his trousers were rolled up the blades of his shins. As I opened a second bottle and the foam spilled across the warped floorboards, I asked him "Why did you kill Carter?"

The Russian chewed his lower lip. "Why do *you* suspect that I did?"

"Your *Inquiry into Some Points of Seamanship*. I don't read Russian, but I know the name Harry when I see it in a margin. You've been to this station before. Did he interrupt you, stealing?"

Junker sipped his drink, staring at the effervescence. "I have. Yes—I have been here—a lot. It wasn't suicide. I knew

Harry, well. I didn't need to steal from him. Your nigger in uniform was here before, also. Did you know that?"

"I know. Why did you lie about it?"

"I was not asleep, you understand, while the three of you were talking on the boat. I was listening to you, very carefully. The cannibal and the half-caste couldn't translate sufficiently. But the fact is that he was close—I heard his mention of the rival. The man is a privateer, I should say. That is who murdered Carter."

"You were a witness."

"No, not quite. I ran away. When I saw your steamer, I thought I could return with you, to the station. Then, I would know for certain that he was dead, but you knew already. I only *heard* the shot, you see—" The nameless privateer had been poaching Company ivory for months. "That night, I saw him walking nonchalantly out of the forest, into the station. He wears the Company uniform. He looked to be unarmed. Carter opened the door and they spoke for a few minutes upon the threshold, framed in the lamplight from inside, two shadows. The privateer held up his hand, thus, in surrender. They went inside and Carter closed the door. They talked, I suppose, and had words. At first, I saw Carter ushering the privateer out of the station building with his shotgun pressed into the man's spine. Then, in the moonlight, I saw that the man with the gun was not Carter. As they were about to disappear into the tree line, Carter wheeled on the man and they began to struggle. Carter cried out, and I ran." Junker looked away, fascinated with a moth that was beating its powdery wings against an oil lamp.

Later, with Junker then retired to his hut, Devlin slogging ashamedly downriver, and the station washed by a gauzy rain, I lay upon my back, staring at the planks of the ceiling. It was an oceanic peace that settled within me, my spine a compass needle becalmed between tender poles, my nerves impalpable, ghostly filaments. Without agitation, I fell through unknown depths toward the absolute black stillness that existed before the protests of space and time—all of this, on a wire-spring bed, hymned by phantoms of rain. With this freelance killer roaming with his coterie somewhere outside the station, I should not have experienced such peace, yet I was not afraid. I had come home. Exhaustion slid like a dead monkey from my shoulders. The boas of cramp relinquished my legs. My lungs pulled at the glittering, angelic air. It must be close to two years since that night.

*Swallowed a dozen grains of calomel—ivory writhing in the night—men pushed the dead elephant into the river—*When we discovered our first elephants, they were bathing in a thin vein of ivy-colored water, two males, five females and a calf. The eldest bull was massive, yet showed signs of emaciation after the fracturing of his last eyeteeth. Leaving the stream, he lanced and smashed with the trees with his ancient tusks, the bright foliage cascading over his sunken back. The lips of his trunk foraged for the softest leaves. The younger male looked to weigh about six tonnes. He must have been new to this group, seeking a mate. Nsumbu pointed out the matriarch, the silvery-brown cow that led the herd. She was a yard shorter than the stud and half as heavy. The cows were patiently shadowing the oldest bull toward his death, spiraling through the forest, and this adolescent had inter-rupted their melancholy walk. Measured against the bulls, with impressive tusks of their own, the organized maternity was overwhelming. The calf shambled between them, lolling its trunk, cooling its wrinkled skin with busy, membranous ears. We tracked them for about two miles, until they were about to emerge onto an open plain of yellow-brown grass.

We had moved slightly ahead of their flank, so that where the jungle doglegged, we could shoot at them from a natural hide in the cane break. There were six of us in the front rank and six more behind. The Martini-Henry .303 being too light for these giants, I took aim at them with a Remington four bore. We waited until they were no more than twenty-five yards away. The earth shuddered beneath their feet. Pale adrenaline washed through me, and at last, I called out the order. Our first fusillade struck the elephants, head on. The slugs shattered their front shields of their crania, blowing splinters back into the brain. Some shots found the hose of the trachea or the wet funnel behind an eye. An impossible sound erupted from them as we reloaded, and the wounds projected their blood like pistons. They wheeled and crashed against each other in a titanic knot of terror, confusion, pain and mutilation. The matriarch charged us, even as a section of her cheek hung in a desecrated flap, an artery pumping crimson flashes over her front legs. Nsumbu fired at her, blasting a fist-sized lump of brain out of the side of her shaking head. Wild-eyed, he shoved another slug into the breach. They collapsed slowly like gray buildings under artillery, the architecture of their flesh and bone resisting, swaying stubbornly and yet helplessly under our attack. The elder male fell first, his tusks gouging the wet earth in two long furrows. Into these extrusions, he coughed the last of his life. The others, brains blown out, trunks severed and ears ripped by our five volleys, lay about him, heaving and expiring under the gunpowder sky. The calf lay dead with them, shot pointlessly behind the ear. Nsumbu and the rest hurried toward them with machetes and picks, excising the ivory from the pitiful corpses. A mountain of withering gray flesh awaited the birds and the hyenas. Between the dozen of us in the hunting party, we bore nine hundred pounds of ivory back to the station. Fires burned in the early evening, and Johnny Malebo, Junker and the Negroes who had remained greeted us, Malebo handing me a quinine pill and a glass of gin. My clothes were stiff with blood. Malebo had fixed up my hammock as I had requested of him, and when I fell into it, I sobbed.

My inimical Rival did not even begin to reveal himself for several weeks, no doubt cautious at seeing the station occupied again. But the fleeting sensations of being watched reported by Johnny Malebo as he further trained the blacks in our business were shared and undeniable. The whites of eyes flickered in the bush—twigs cracked. At times, the tree line would breathe, tense and suspicious. We gathered ivory at a decent rate, cleaning the tall curved teeth, and amassing our pallid stockpile. Devlin's retreat from the river left another hole in the company, and it was the spy, Émile, who replaced the missing link in the ivory chain, piloting a steamboat up to my station toward the end of the second month. In some ways, it was a relief to see him. His flat sculling craft was almost overwhelmed by our cull.

"This is more than we had from Carter in six months," he observed.

"Perhaps we're not being harried as he was."

I invited Émile to my barracks, to give him an hour of respite from the smothering concentration he would have to summon to avoid scuttling his boat in the morass of barbs and snares concealed beneath the surface. As we traipsed up the hill to my station house, I glimpsed Junker disappearing behind a shadowed sap tree. Ushering Émile inside, I closed the door and called for Nsumbu to brew tea and prepare the service.

Lowering his chin, and raising his eyes under his brows, Émile watched him adding leaves to the pot. "How is he working out?" His voice was a conspiratorial whisper, even though he knew that Nsumbu would not understand most of the words spoken between us.

"Nsumbu is *ya mbóté*," I said, deliberately wrecking the spy's assumed sphere of confidence. Nsumbu fastened the top button of his Company jacket, his expression warm and self-assured.

"Excellent news," Émile continued, speaking openly. "I am certain that you are all making spectacular progress." He flashed a smile at my *boyi,* an acknowledgement that he wanted to express morally, and emotionally, but that was nonetheless difficult for him physically. He had never smiled so unguardedly at a Negro before, and it cost him. There was a gentle tremor in his bearded cheek.

We drank our tea and Émile described the tedium at Léopoldville. In all the time that he was sitting with me, with Nsumbu working in the background, he seemed unable to find comfort, in his chair, or inside his skin. He was like a nervous man, too close to his dreams. Lifting one of my porcelain cups to his lips, the handle snapped off, and the vessel smashed on the floorboards between his feet. Émile was left holding only a delicate curl of bone white. Nsumbu crouched, plucking up the shards—an image of broken, sepia boat.

"Makes you feel funny, being where a fellow killed himself." He was testing me.

"I'm indifferent to it now, as cold as that makes me appear."

"No, no . . . I quite understand. One must soldier on. I'll be back for another consignment in—what—another month?"

"We'll look forward to it."

Native tobacco—green visions—an ivory crucifix floats downstream—Nsumbu woke me. In the light from the candle he clutched in his fingers, he was distraught, insensible to the hot wax rolling in pearl beads over his wrist.

"Malangu kafua!" Spittle clung to his teeth as he struggled to make me understand him. *"Dead!"* He was pulling me by the wrists to get out of bed. Lighting an oil lamp, I went with him, barefoot and shirtless into the night. We did not have to go far. Nsumbu pointed the way. Malangu's body lay contorted in the grass, about a dozen yards behind the station house. There was a bullet hole between his eyebrows and the crown of his inky head was missing. In the lamplight, the last clot of brain clung to the scalp like an evicted hermit crab. Nsumbu got to his knees, rubbing the naked chest, touching the throat, massaging the final sparks of the man's soul out of the decimated skin. I knelt beside him, also. It was then that I made an appalling discovery. There was a piece of paper stuffed inside Malangu's skull. Putting my right arm around Nsumbu's trembling shoulder, I reached into the shattered bone with my left hand. Without reading it, I tucked the paper inside the waist of my pajamas. We could not leave him where he lay, so we shrouded him in one of my sheets and took him inside the station house, where the corpse hardened and reeked in the corner. When I was alone that morning, before speaking with anyone else, I examined the note. "Render therefore unto Caesar the things which are Caesar's—and unto God the things that are God's." Silently, I made my way to the Russian's hut. He was inside, sleeping in his rags, his navigation manual resting upon his chest. I raised my revolver and took aim at that pale face with its blepharitis and sunburned features, wishing that I had the certainty that I needed to squeeze the trigger. I held the gun there for several minutes. It was useless. Returning to my quarters, I comforted Nsumbu as well as I was able. As dawn approached, quite drunk and with barely enough light, we dug a grave and lowered Malangu down into the hungry brown soil. He had been with us on the first ivory expedition. Had the Rival been watching us, then? He must have been abducted from the station and murdered at some distance, for none of us heard the gun shot. The station was profoundly disturbed by Malangu's murder, not least of all Johnny Malebo who came to me racked with doubts. "I'm in a bind, Kurtz," he said. His voice was thinned by hysteria. "Look at me. I bet he'll only kill a few more of our fellows to make his point, but where do I stand? I'm part nigger, and I'll confess to you that the white part of me is afraid of it. I've been in here too long. I could see Yorkshire, but my luck is running out. If a bullet or a spear doesn't get me, then the sleeping sickness will. And as for my conscience—my conscience is dismembered by horses." He picked at an angry mosquito bite on his cheek. Outside, some of the men were singing beside Malangu's grave. Malebo steadied himself. "I want out."

It was convenient to imagine myself walking into the jungle and discovering the Rival, like Stanley finding Livingstone, two near-dead men united by some cordial accident. Yet, I knew that it could not be that way. We were, all of us—*In a pestilential prison with a life-long lock, Awaiting the sensation of a short, sharp shock*—There was nothing to be gained in waiting for him to come to me. I resolved to go after him, to run him down as quickly as possible. I had Nsumbu bring the Russian to my quarters, and there we gagged him and then, after removing the mattress, bound him to my metal bed frame. He struggled like an eel for a moment, before I pushed a laudanum-soaked rag into his face. I could not have him interfering. Nsumbu would administer the anesthetic again if Junker awoke and resisted. Otherwise, Nsumbu would sit in the corner with a Martini-Henry. I made a bargain with Johnny Malebo. He would help me get rid of the Rival, and I would help him get out of the

Company, when it was done. I promised the half-caste that it would be his final act in uniform.

I understood now something that had been obscure to me since my arrival at the station. It was the presence of this Rival, and the reputation of his malevolence that had confined the Negroes here, even after Carter's death, when they might reasonably have sought to return to their villages. The station on the river, and the assumption that it would be reclaimed for the Company, were ironic securities against the marauder and his messianic violence. He never took the station for himself, because he did not require it, and couldn't use it, anyway. He might have burned it to the ground, I suppose. If he were shipping ivory, it was being done in an unorthodox fashion. It was almost inconceivable that he would bring it out by land. As Malebo said, "But then, a man like that—" The two of us searched for his encampment through turbid waves of heat. Lightning burst in the dry afternoon sky. We tracked east, and then southeast, discovering the carcass of a bull elephant beside a swamp, and some evidence of the retreat of the men who had killed it. The sockets where the ivory had been were like molasses studded with flies. Dogs had hollowed out its huge body. Machetes had cleared the branches near to it, and the path was littered with a dented tobacco tin, and then a broken wine bottle and other detritus as we followed it. After an hour, beside a megalithic stone, we discovered a dead Negro sprawled in the undergrowth. Part of his face was missing where he had been shot through the jaw, and his naked body bore the marks of having been beaten by a furious mob. As I examined him, I saw that both of his hands had been amputated, white bone branching out of his scarlet wrists. The removal of his hands and the bloating of his body from so many blows clearly meant nothing to his killers, except as a prelude to his execution. The grass was tacky with his blood. Malebo vomited against the rock. I asked him how long he thought the man had been dead.

Malebo straightened. "Two hours, perhaps three. I wonder what the poor bugger did to offend him?"

"It doesn't matter, does it? This man means to destroy us all, one way or another. Let's go."

Scarecrows impale the desolate bush—hung with tendrils of wool—amulets shimmer in the rain—At dusk, we detected the aromas of a fire pit and flesh cooking over it. The far-reaching smoke came to us long before we could hear, or observe the encampment, but it led us in. There was something careless or arrogant about this man. In fading light, we came stealthily to the rim of the clearing where the Rival waited. Three of his gang surrounded the fire, turning a spit over the red flames. To the right of these was a green canvas tent, a man's shadow cast against the fabric by the striking of a match. The tusks of the dead bull elephant lay on the ground outside it, marking the threshold. We were lucky. The dead man on the trail narrowed our odds. I wondered, could his retinue really be of four, now three, or were there others, waiting for his return? As my eyes adjusted to the firelight, I saw that the thing on the spit had been a man. The jackal-drawn men sliced at the scorched skin with their knives. I whispered the word, and Malebo and I fired on them. His rifle blasted the ribs out of one of them, and as they stood rigid in the orange embers rolling turbulently from the half-eaten corpse, I took the other two with three shots from my revolver. The Rival remained in his tent. I called out: "You're surrounded, man! Resist us, and there will be fifty bullets in you before you can lift your arm." A gun was thrown out from the tent. "No tricks," I said. We saw the embers of a cigarette extended through the flap before our enemy crawled awkwardly over the white tusks and, kneeling, cigarette in mouth, raised his hands in surrender. "My God," I said. Without volition, I dropped to my knees in front of him, meeting his eyes. He looked older, his face thinner than before, and his scalp bore the fresh cut marks of close shaving. "What are you doing here, Paine?" That smile cut through all the savagery of the night and magnified it beyond comprehension. There is a risk, for me, in recollecting it. The crone moves toward the blinds . . .

When Tacitus followed the Rhine north into the iron forests of the Aryans, he saw black-daubed savages, white men painted in the sullen shade of Hell. And in his ride through the gothic pines, chasms and peaks, he was yet impressed with the assemblies of justice and the governance of the barbaric places he crossed. Snows weighted the trees and mud immersed him in the melt. He watched trials that ended in floggings and hangings. He observed the slow deliberations of all the spear-waving tribes of Germany. His own father had been a slave, and Tacitus never permitted himself to forget the shadow he had emerged from. Through camps of midnight-colored primitives, he admired them. Under the bronze bondage of Rome, he pitied them. Later, in Africa, he set his soft voice against the corrupt. Remember, my father was from the Rhineland Ashkenazi, and in the unscrewing of ancient time in the north of Europe, perhaps some ancestor of mine had painted himself like a cannibal to intimidate Tacitus and his mare in a dark green glade. I would set the trial of Eric Paine, my nemesis. What was it Dadd had said at Broadmoor? The end of every civilization comes from the river. It was not merely Paine who would be on trial, but the whole repugnant enterprise. After returning to Chatham in 1881, Eric Paine had gone like a whirlwind through his ivory pension. Finding himself on

Queer Street with a rising tide of debt showing no sign of finding its high water mark, he returned to the Congo, the one place on earth where he could cancel out his losses. Thinking himself short of time, he required this lightless place, unimpeded by conscience and law. He brought with him the ruthless pillaging instincts of his race. In truth, there would be no trial, only a judgment. I had now my chance to kill Mephistopheles, to shut down the Faustian theater for good. I would step back from the pit of Hell and be revealed, a New Man. Inasmuch as Eric Paine and my sins could not be uncoupled, I would proffer them no mercy. I would be as pitiless and relentless with his flesh as the vicious messenger had been with my grieving soul. He must have known that he had won it cheaply—sixteen years old, dragging my mother's coffin through the shale and muddy sand of Calais, abandoned just moments before by the man who killed her, who killed Édouard Kurtz, the boy. Eric Paine swooped, a hawk from the miserable sky of my melancholy. He was a splinter of my father. He was a truant ghost to set my mind on its edge, and he watched it rolling from the wet iron deck of the steamer into the sea beneath the White Cliffs of Dover. I realize now that from that moment I never truly touched land again until I touched Africa. Everything else can be lied about, but not this.

There were five of us in the grove: Malebo, Nsumbu, Junker, Paine, and myself. "Kibila!" Nsumbu called it, anointing it by wiping his sweat on the leaves that encircled us. Junker had good reason to be nervous.

"'Ello, Nikolai," Paine said. "You stayed, after all. Fancy that . . ."

"Shut up," I said. "Do you think that I hadn't noticed that *this*"—I grabbed the Russian by the shoulder, clutching a section of quilted red satin—"this is from Carter's smoking jacket. Now, don't you bloody move, Junker, or I'll blow your brains out. Johnny!" Nsumbu had the noose around Paine's neck. "I'll do it," I said, taking the rope from him, and throwing the length of it over a strong bough. I took the slack and walked Paine up onto his toes, as the noose chewed his throat and stretched his neck. Malebo raised his rifle, training the barrel only inches from the Russian's cheek. Junker began whimpering, a high-pitched hunger, frightened little bat squeaks. The rope over the bough rained thin shavings of bark, creaking as I lifted Paine from his feet. He grabbed at the rope, kicking and gargling. A stream of amber urine spread at his groin. Yet, wanting him alive for a while longer, I lowered him again, until he could support his weight under the improvised winch. He coughed and retched bile over his chest. Standing close to him, I said, "You're not going back to Chatham, Eric." Then I hauled him up on the gallows again, watching his eyes cloud, suspending him above the lice and delicate flowers of the jungle floor. When I lowered him a second time, he was almost dead. The rope burned my palms. "You can be honest with us, Nikolai . . ." I left an opening and he walked through it.

"Kurtz, please—he made me do it." The Russian lowered his chin, pressing it tight against his collarbone, shaking under the shadow of Johnny Malebo's rifle. "I killed Carter, but it was against my will. *Please*—" His voice was a cracked whisper, a death rattle.

"Did you hear that, Eric? Nikolai has confessed to killing Harold Carter. Isn't that extraordinary?"

A rictus of pleasure warped the Rival's bloodless face. He tried to speak, but was inaudible, heaving under the slow pressure of the rope. His neck began to crack.

"It seems unfair to hang you." I let the rope go, and his body slumped to the ground. "Help him up, Nsumbu." I made a gesture. Nsumbu lifted Paine to his knees. I watched him swaying in the tubes of sunlight. I loosened the noose, almost gratefully, patting his cheek as one might a spent horse. Stepping behind Paine, I looked at the Russian in his incriminating rags. "All right, Nikolai." As Junker raised his eyes, I took the shaving blade from my pocket. I dug my fingers into Eric Paine's slick brow and drew the shining razor across his throat. I cried out at the livid blue sky, cutting and cutting until the head came away from the neck. The lava of his blood sprayed the trees.

She stood up, letting the black wool fall from her skeletal knees. *No!* The razor was in my hand, my body drenched in blood—elephantine screams cracking the glass that looked out on the sparkling tomb streets of Brussels—*It is cruel of me, so unspeakably cruel. Not now!*—Black stripes cascaded through my eyes as the crone extended her mottled skin toward the venetian blinds. I stood alone at the lightless rim of the universe, petrified. It was so cold there. All that I had to do was to look back, over my shoulder, but I was too afraid. The breath of solar winds made ice on my collar, crystals spread along my jaw. My throat ached with it. There was a voice behind me. "Did you know that Tambov in Russian means 'abyss'?" It was Nikolai Junker. I turned my head, my vertebrae grinding, and diamonds of sweat running over my skin. Tasting salt, I saw only darkness. Slowly, I began to recede from the rim, slipping away without any sense of my weight. Filaments of light pricked the forbidding distance as I accelerated, until I was a cannonball of shivering, fevered flesh. The pinpricks of light were a galaxy, a city on jet-black water—Inordinately, I fell—

The Russian stood over me, holding a bowl of hot broth. I was in my bunk. His blue eyes swiveled, studying me, as he raised a spoon to my lips. "At first, I thought the coma had got you. Three days—" I saw the quilted red satin on his shoulder, ripped threads where I had grabbed him. It was hard to open my mouth, and the soup spilled along my cheek. "It can't have been the sleeping sickness, then." I tried to speak, but my throat was filled with spines and needles. I moved my head to say no. Junker raised the spoon again, and I managed to take some of it. It was extremely salty. "I've seen this before. I am sorry for you, Kurtz."

"Where is it?"

"What?"

"Eric Paine's head."

*On all fours—memories washing away—station overgrown with ivory—*When Émile returned for more ivory, some weeks later, we hurried him, barely letting him off the boat, most inhospitably. He was quite put out, and glared at me as though I had committed some personal betrayal of him, the details of which the spy could not divine, yet it was there, nagging at him in the fly-buzz over the tepid water. He was soon distracted, however, by the haul of giant tusks from the station, curved and brilliant white on his deck. The cost of all this to the half-caste was profound. Honorably, he had tried to remain silent while I recovered myself, but it was corrosive to him. That evening, after Émile had gone back downriver, Malebo and I sat upon the empty jetty. "If I had shot the Russian—" he said, his naked feet dangling in the water. "I don't mean that you would have died from your fever. I mean that I would have become—like you. Although, it seems that you've forgiven Junker, so there's something in you." I tried to smile. Malebo said, "Look, we agreed that you would help me get out of here. I've tried to wait until you are well again. I know I could have gone back with the ivory this time, but it seemed wrong, somehow. It's the strangest thing. I want to abandon you, but part of me cannot. I think I should go back on the next boat. I know that you're not an evil man, Kurtz, but what you did: that was the final straw for me in this godforsaken country. I think I might admire you, but I can't go on." Émile must have become ill, for he did not return on time, and evidently, the Company had not yet assigned a replacement for Devlin, or the spy. The ivory stacked up, fossilizing for two months. Malebo would stand staring at it in despair.

Nsumbu has dreams of returning to London with me, where he will be a *sapeur,* dressed in a peacock suit, strutting with an ivory cane, a golden monocle in his eye. He imagines that we will trawl the opium dens of Limehouse together, slumbering in luxuriant folds of dragon scales. He asks me what white women look like, and I describe what I can recall of you. I don't want to tell him that I am never going back, or that my skin admits me, pays my entrance, while his skin denies him. I think that he must know this, but has come to perceive me as some exception to the order of things. We smoked a little hemp this evening. His benighted eyes glittered with something, as though he too were witness to that city I had seen in the hurtling fragments of my death.

*Bees from a smoking tree—hands on bloodstained drums— memories of the Rhine—*The body had been preserved in a brine of salt and river water. Some of the tacky blood was contained in a flask made from a stiffened animal bladder wrapped in feline pelt. Nsumbu directed me to a pile of oily banana leaves and palm leaves, folded into rhomboid parcels. Inside these, through the gaps in the leaves, the roasted tatters of my enemy emitted a ghostly steam. For my part, I brought several bottles of champagne and some porter beer, splashing these into my tea service that I shared with the glorious Negroes that shared the *kibila* with us. The clearing was obscured with smoke, but still I think I saw a yellowish star fall through the vault between the trees. There were not enough porcelain cups to go around, so tin substitutes and empty shell casings from my four-bore Remington were employed as champagne flutes. Soon, the men were drunk, and we passed the bloody flask and shoveled the body of Eric Paine into our hungry mouths, each of us dripping crimson in spectral moonlight. Then, we sliced our palms and shared our consanguine pulse together in one beautiful primitive convulsion of kinship. They had never seen a white man eat another man, let alone another white man—the complexion of my station was forever changed. I chewed with venom. We danced in the macabre embers, and, beating the earth with his blue Company jacket, Nsumbu cried out: "Danse! Danse! Danse! Danse!" Other men slapped their skin drums and the wild percussion exploded—cannon-shot through the fevered gloom.

When She departed tonight, I imagined that I was watching the station from a vertiginous height—the three of us, She, Nsumbu and I forming a prism, a triangle of dangerous ectoplasm imprinted upon the jungle, sharp angles countering the serpentine river. I was a falcon that could not resist its lure, tethered. The bloat of her belly says that She is pregnant.

Torrents of rain—seen from the profound reaches of fever—smashed huts—With no relief forthcoming, and the ivory diminishing, I ordered that pontoons be built so that it could be taken back to the central station. With the current, we could manage to guide the cargo downriver in canoes. The construction of the pontoons was arduous, requiring the felling of several trees. The platforms had to be big to displace the weight of the ivory. Fortunately, there were several empty oil drums at the station and these air filled canisters made the transit possible. And so, we travelled with our precious and precarious haul, lashed to the pontoons. We carried provisions in our crude dugouts and made as good time as we were able in the punishing heat. Each of us had two Negroes in our boats. On the second day, I had to shoot a hippopotamus in his bulbous snout as he threated to overturn us. Crocodiles arrowed through the marshy reeds and tore into the floating bulk as its gore flowed out behind it. Otherwise, the navigation itself was quite uneventful, only the tedium of a seemingly endless ebb.

At first, it gave me no pleasure to libel Johnny Malebo to Montagu at the central station and the Company ombudsmen, yet it was a means to an end. However, by the time we reached Léopoldville, my position and sympathy for him changed. Malebo had seen the note and approved it, so that he knew where he stood: "Clear this poor devil out of the country, and don't bother sending me more of that sort. I had rather be alone than have the kind of men you can dispose of with me." He paddled in a desultory manner, a man staring through the flimsy scenery of his fate, seeking the hand behind it. The note was sealed in an envelope in his breast pocket. He had the aspect of an asylum inmate, waiting for another arbitrary disappoint-ment, a blanched, fearful expression. I had seen that caste on men as they walked toward the iron gates of Broadmoor, limping toward the free world. Insects swarmed about him on the surface of the water. The fear of a fever on the way out held his spine in a fist. He swatted at the flies with his hand, trying not to release his oar. Finally, he stopped paddling altogether, and his men glanced at one another before doing the same. I came alongside him to discover the matter. The insects shifted to another section of the river.

"I saw it, you know?" he said in a stricken, insinuating tone.

"So what?" The paddle dripped pleasantly across my shins.

"Why don't you give it up?" he said. "Insist on escorting me as far as Boma. You could get on a ship. In a month, you could be back in England. Come north with me. We're all keeping secrets now. Junker helped you out of your malaise, so you'll never tell that he murdered Carter, and I think I understand you there: what good would it do? Now I . . ." He trailed off, unable to announce what he had witnessed.

"That's blackmail, Johnny."

"Kurtz! Why should you be lost? You're getting me out. No one needs to know what happened."

"That's not a condition in my having you extracted," I said. The banks of the central station were visible, as were the hillside with the flagpole where Émile and I had talked. "I can imagine that you'll hurry up to Montagu's hut to inform him that Kurtz is a cannibal. That will spoil his appetite, again. He won't thank you for the outlandish gossip. With that said, his spy might enjoy chewing on the rumor, if he's still alive, that is. You know, that's rather good." The prospect made me laugh at him. "Still, there's little but gossip and fossils left at Léopoldville."

"Don't mock me."

"So, that's it? I libel you because you ask me to, and then you slander me from Stanley Pool to Brussels because you can't stand that I have discovered the only reasonable solution to the Company? Your white half is in full revolt. The fight for albescence—it's like cancer. Jesus Christ, Johnny. I should shoot you between your divided eyes, before it's too late. I'll tell you what: you tell Montagu whatever you wish. It doesn't mean anything to me, anymore. But do me this favor." I reached inside my shirt. "I've got some letters here, for *The Daily Telegraph*, for *The Times* and *The Manchester Guardian*. You see that they get through, all right? Are such things done on Albion's shores?"

As the current drew us toward the bank, I ordered the two Negroes from his dugout into mine and demanded that Malebo give me whatever was left of the rations he carried. From my seat at the stern, I cut the rope that attached me to the pontoons of ivory. "Kuvutuka, station!" I said it as best as I could, pointing back upriver, whence we had come. The four black men began paddling away, as Malebo and the ivory drifted further toward the jetties of the central station, where a crowd of men assembled to gather the cargo. As I made inventory of our remaining provisions, the channel swallowed us again, and I felt the humid embrace of the mangroves narrowing. Distantly, I fancied that I could hear the half-caste cursing me from the iron pier. When we returned to the station, starving and exhausted, Nikolai Junker was gone. These disappearances of his would be frequent. He would abscond to his rotting hut of reeds, then return, obsequious as the lapdog he truly was, and as he remains, even as I sit here writing this.

*Wild figs—algae on the oblong paddle blades—the setting sun splashing my death on the horizon—*Standing at the river's edge, I held the cartridge box in both hands, watching a bird of prey arc over the swamps. Within the shrill clamoring of monkeys, the awakening peacocks, the rasping bark of silver hyenas and the bellowing of the buffalos, I opened the latch and stared at the tear-stained contents. These were the documents that proved my existence—all forgeries. As the morning's steam formed over the gilded water, I waded in. My naked feet were subsumed in silt. There was a faint ringing in my ears. Gripping the metal box in the crook of my arm, I picked out the papers one by one, sowing my past upon a mosquito-clouded shimmer. It was here that I changed my mind about returning any photograph of myself to you, and that single image fell into the channel. My false fragments floated away from me, their inks diffusing as the stationary began to disintegrate. A history was dismembered, disembodied from its host. Dropping the empty canister, I recalled Dadd's obscure warning about jealousy and the iron maiden, how his god went in shreds and tatters down the Nile, betrayed. I found myself laughing at it all. Watching my identity on the water, the empty box floating after it, was a suicide, an epiphany. I released the things that pretended to be Kurtz. After these, I threw my watch into a swirl of weed. When I returned to my quarters, I smashed Harold Carter's mantel clock, kicking the brittle mechanism into the corners of the room, crushing the pearlescent face. I had escaped. I had escaped and found a god in my shadow, rippling on the Congo. And so I began disentangling my station from the laggardly auspices of the Company. As the Minotaur discovering the cheating twine of Ariadne—that is, you, my Intended—stretched around the pitch angles of my home, I cut it with my horns, and I reestablished my labyrinth around me. I mounted the contorted resinous head of Eric Paine upon a sharpened pole at the perimeter. His empty eyes shriveled in the sun and shut, entombing blue flies in the braincase. The display of my Rival's head was a civilized gesture, worthy of the monarchies of Europe, beneath the ravens of the Tower of London and the carnivorous doves of the Bastille. Only a hypocrite could behold the head of Paine and deem it retrograde. I went out into the wild bush and sought out his allies, those tribal savages who might yet strive to avenge his death. I wanted no risk. I burned their shanties, and I extinguished mercy. I cut the skinny men down as they fled through the long grass—meatless tangles of the dead littered the bush. For I had resolved to give the Company the excess it desired. The next steamers they sent to my station for my ivory were almost scuttled beneath the mass of tusks. We dropped them contemptuously upon the deck of the new captain, a stocky nothing from Antwerp. The pallid Company men in their sweat-soaked blue uniforms were silent as Nsumbu and our men filed down the slope toward them. I surrounded my station with decapitations, the brown nubs like balls of resin as they deformed, all staring inward toward my house, except for that of Paine, who glared out toward the Congo. Decay rendered his white skin indistinguishable from the cannibal disciples arrayed about him. I admitted the captain from Antwerp three more times, treating him sullenly, as I had done with Émile's final visits. As soon as I could judge that Montagu, Janssens and the others were impressed with me, I established my blockade—a prostitute leading them on before slamming the door on their trembling fingers. The next steamer that struggled in the narrow channel before my station was riddled with spears, its funnel belching smoke as it retreated, agents screaming with panic and superficial wounds. The spears were thrown ostentatiously, without any intent to kill.

The vexatious Junker returned to the station, a brace of fowl slung over his shoulder, a trickle of their blood dried on his pastiche uniform. He had tramped along the bank from his hovel, rendering him wan with dehydration and cramped in the feet, from slipping in the bogs, gripping rocks with his toes. I watched him hobble up the slope between the grass huts, his gait like a man late from a turgid battlefield. It was a simple perception, then, to see all the swatches covering or repairing the plain khaki of the Van Shuyten Expedition as mementos from dead men. He stitched with a surgeon's precision, a steadiness practiced in freezing holds at sea. The manifold fragments of his exterior reflected his mind, a broken window of stained glass. Everything he stole from other men gave evidence that he was alive. His insecurity was palpable. He was a scavenger, a survivor. He leeched on me, and yet, I wondered what fresh damage the judgment of my Rival had done him. Things acted upon Junker anachronistically. But then, is that not the case with every one of us—the scent of a lily exposing some newly agitated laceration of memory and conscience? There were ones like Vicious Boy, whose cruelty lurked beneath the thinnest, most transparent membrane. Then, there were ones like Junker, whose cringing was merely the outward signal of his determination to force his hatred back down inside himself. He was always fighting it. He lived in fear of these dorsal sins bursting from his body.

The fowl we cooked together was reminiscent of good French pheasant. I was grateful for the familiar gray meat and a quiet conversation. We dined as if nothing had happened between us. We planted the colorful feathers in a fringe at the edge of what was becoming my garden, between the sentinel heads. Brushing the soil from our hands, we watched the approach of a rainstorm, a granite streak across the sky coming form the opposite bank, but still far away. He said, "I can hear it." There was pleasure in his red-rimmed eyes. Brushing the soil from our hands, we returned inside. "I was with him for a year," Junker said, staring from my window at the one outward-facing skull. "I don't know if it was some—how shall I say?—charismatic power in him, or some terrible weakness in me, but I was— *persuaded.* Do you believe in devils?" he asked, sipping at a glass of port, licking his lips.

"Sometimes, when it suits me. When I met that man for the first time, I did not. Even now, I wonder if there has ever been a time when I have been certain that he was a man." I felt drunk. "He had a map of this place with him, or some of it, on brilliant white paper. That is what I saw in him, an irrational conduit to a better place."

"A better place?" Junker scoffed. "This?"

"Eric Paine *was* the Company. In his way, *in its way,* it exploited a moment in me. How many others must Leopold have Shanghaied? I can see it now as the cosh to the back of the head that it was. I had my first seizure in Eric Paine's presence. He vanished on me during that blackout. Now I understand it. The fits returned as I came closer to discovering him again. They came back in Matadi."

"He was close to Matadi. I was with him. He wanted to observe any progress on the railway. He was afraid of it. It threatened his sense of dominion, and—"

I interrupted him. "Bloody Hell, Nikolai! I'm not having any more of this. Listen to us: seduced by dull specters simply because those specters are silent. We've become sentimental, investing so much in false idols and stolen goods. Damn Eric Paine. Damn them all."

"Tell me," the Russian urged, pouring us another drink, "What did he taste like when you *ate* him?"

"Nothing."

"Aha! Because he wasn't real!"

"Shut up. No. He was real, all right. But *my* reality is ascendant."

Junker picked a thorn out of his sleeve. "My clothes are always getting torn. You see, this is what happens when you venture off the path. But, if you've killed a man, you'd better stick to the briar as much as you can. Did Carter have children?"

I lied: "I don't know. What could you do, anyway?"

"If you let me, I could send them some ivory."

"I wouldn't let you. I don't need any thorns in my crown, Nikolai. But perhaps you should send some to Van Shuyten."

The rain thundered across the roof as I got up to brew coffee. The Russian wandered about and picked up my *Report on the Suppression of Savage Customs.* He spoke sarcastically. "Not really doing much to suppress savagery, are you?"

"Why should I?"

He shrugged his shoulders, the red satin imprint of Harold Carter stitched to him. "If you want to play god, who are any of us to argue?"

I did not answer him.

Sometimes, I wonder if She is slowly poisoning me. I saw her tonight, her belly round as an eclipsed sun. She set in my mind the thought of crawling to my Pit and lying down with my earthworms, my centipedes, and my snails traversing my ivory, to die. How can a man be so susceptible to other people? I walked outside with my revolver and a large Gordon's and quinine, concentrating on washing any tincture of her from my guts, watching the tree line, listening to symphonies of rain-smashed orchids and creaking rubber. If things got to be too much, I could always trepan my hairless skull with a bullet. Do you ever imagine yourself collapsing from the outside in, a little implosion of tired skin? I do.

I am riding a bull elephant into the foyer of the Victoria. The Portuguese *maître d'hôtel* is impaled on the right tusk of my animal. The crystal chandelier has been smashed from its plaster ceiling rose and fragments of glass spill across the checkered floor tiles like hailstones. Two old men in dinner suits attempt to rise from a green baize table where they were playing blackjack, before spears shatter the windows and pin them to the mildewed wallpaper, viscera eloping along the wooden shafts. As I rein my elephant into the high-ceilinged ballroom, the Portuguese grabs hopelessly at the ivory running through his intestines and out of his back. Rubber plants overturn out of red clay urns. The piano is destroyed, scattering ivory keys. At last, he slips off the tusk as I trample the soporific diners. My elephant sways its massive gray head in *musth*—a sound like the trumpets of the Apocalypse. The French doors to the hothouse are dashed to smithereens, the panes lacerating a Company man in a tuxedo, slicing off the side of his face. He is still holding a champagne flute in his left hand as I blow the arm off with my four-bore. As I destroy the hothouse, a wail of triumph goes up, filling the blue air outside. Twenty niggers on twenty elephants brandish spears and rifles. They soak the hotel in kerosene. This is how we wage war, my putsch against the Company. Far behind us, the Congo languishes beneath a vast plume of threatening smoke, the whites evicted even from their very graves. Elephants smash the headstones of the Léopoldville cemetery, uprooting the splintering coffins with their tusks, and throwing the desecrated skeletons over their shoulders as simply as a superstitious woman throws salt at the Devil. The stations are decimated—dead accountants bleed out into the amber waters. I tear up the Matadi railway track and block the channel with sunken wrecks, sinking every boat. The smoke follows us up through the slave docks of the coast. Cities of terror depopulate before us. I raid camel trains and possess water. I hijack a ferry across the Strait of Gibraltar, and my war elephants traverse the Pyrenees into France. I drive them on through Charleville, laying waste to the house of my birth, and on, northeast into Belgium. It is called the Siege of Brussels. A million Africans fall in

behind me, a great funnel of war, an exodus of negritude—
La guerre contre la raison, contre fantômes et les ombres—
Fire runs through the marble balustrades like lava. The
palace of the colonists collapses in glowing timbers and
broken stone.

I cut off the King's head with a straight razor.

I am worshipped in the Congo when I return.

It is a long time since I have written. With Eric Paine dead
and devoured, there should have been no more seizures. The
second at my station occurred months later. It happened on
the lawn as I was taking tea with Nsumbu and Junker. I
remember that we were walking with our cups and saucers
down toward the riverbank, and I recall something of our
conversation about the jetty rotting. I did not have time
to resist it. Nsumbu told me that a moment before I fell,
I opened my mouth slightly and laughed without making
a sound—I was alone in a humid cave of flesh, mining
miles and years into the future. Fallopian garlands hung
from ancient bone and ivory, dropping scarlet petals.
Thin worms of spermatozoid jelly drifted like plankton
through the clinging air. The scents of creation were overwhelming, an aphrodisiac of pheromones and perspiration, entering me through my skin and issuing through my
lungs, thick, wet, and breathable—a landscape of milks and
blood, thrilling tissue, and vast trellises of calcium. Eating
the walls was like eating the pink cells of pomegranate—I
swam out of Junker's morphine after what I am told were
two nights of delirium. At first, I was desolate with disappointment. I should have been cured of my disease. When
I awoke—sweat in a pool beneath my hammock—I put my
hands to my face and wept, while the Russian spooned soup
toward my lips. The Negroes of the station knew what was
happening. They said that I was summoned to the ghosts of

the river and that these were royal travels. I had been seen to die twice, without dying. They had seen their own kind fall into the sleeping sickness and shrivel in tangles of grass. I was different, they said. I was divine, *nzambi*. I told the Russian where I had been, and of my plans to campaign with war elephants, far north into Europe. I presented him with a vision of the Company offices eviscerated, all of the paperwork of empire blowing from the carbon-rimmed windows, secretaries violated and stuck with spears. *Proximity, miscegenation, atmospheres—all of it may alter the structure of your skull*—We would sail in a reed barge into the Thames. "The problem, Kurtz," the Russian said, "is that I do not doubt you." How could he? In my dreaming coma, I had glimpsed him, smothered in a wall of skin, deep, deep in the endless night of my body. And seeing him there, I discovered the truth of his existence: his catastrophic exterior was not the expression of his mind. It was the reflection of mine. We stayed awake until dawn. I cannot record everything that I said here, in case it should fall into enemy hands. But, I explained to Junker that I saw myself returning to my mother's city, years hence, perhaps during the year and the month of Queen Victoria's Diamond Jubilee. Every street would be hung with Imperial pennants. Jubilant crowds would pour into the streets, clamor at her palace and rumble in her public houses. There would be flags, singing, and pearl buttons. There would be cannon fire, Horseguards parades, salutes and tattoos. Westminster Abbey would ring with golden choruses, shifting sunlit dust from the buttresses. New coins would be struck. Newspapers would ripple with her fifty years upon her throne, and the ink would stain the people with gray streaks, even as she herself was streaked with ashes in her soul. Through the colic of the cold tide, my great barge would sail. My elephants and African warriors would be arrayed on the golden deck, and the Cockneys would cheer for us before they could understand that we were bringing death to the city, gutting the marble vaults, setting the bridges aflame. I would visit your father's house and throw him screaming from his mullioned window. You might stand horrified in the corner of the room, but how would I recognize you now? I have come too far.

"Did you love her?" the Russian asked.

I thought of you then, penetrating the tall grass with your muscular black legs, how you followed me to the Pit and we crawled inside the subterranean crater sprawled with exotic pelts and champagne bottles, surrounded by my ivory, and the peacock-fanned throne of tusks where we consummated one million years of lust. How ardently I wanted you to bulb with my child—

I had not seen it until then. There was a new fragment of cloth sewn over his heart. The stitches were catgut-black. "Goodness, such treachery, Nikolai." I climbed from the hammock, my eyes fixed on the fragment of Paine, pulsing over the Russian's breast. I should have killed him then, but of course, I could not. I struck him down and kicked his pale face. His head made a dull sound against the side of my desk. "I couldn't help it!" he said. "Please!" He scrambled toward the door. As I moved to pursue him, the opiates he had administered wrapped tentacles around my limbs. The door swung on its hinges, clattering against the frame. Daylight flashed through the narrowing gap. I found him some hours later, cowering inside the reed hut below the station, the place downriver where I had first encountered him. He was naked, picking at his clothes with the tip of a scalpel, sweating as he excised the fragments of Harold Carter and Eric Paine from his uniform. His navigation book with its Cyrillic marginalia lay on the floor beside him. As my shadow fell across him from the doorway, he looked up. "I didn't run away from you, you understand? I had forgotten my book here, and I needed it." He pulled a small pencil from behind his ear, licking the lead before adding a new entry. I asked him what he wrote. "It says: Kurtz needs me to watch the station while he assembles his black army." He was right.

Nikolai says that I have a malignancy in my knee of all places.

The following evening, Nsumbu knocked upon my door. I opened the screen to see him grinning in the lamplight. "Mistah Kurtz," he said, extending something toward me. Suddenly, I understood that he was holding a small child in his arms. Pale tendrils of placenta hung from it, as though it were a creature he had retrieved from the river, trailing froth. I studied its small brown face for traces of myself. I remember the thrill of a measure of agony as I realized that the child might have been mine. Had I desired it, secretly? Was there a taint of guilt over my treatment of the half-caste? But, I had done what he wanted. Over Nsumbu's glistening shoulder, She loitered at the perimeter, glimpsed between resinous death masks on their pikes, her fierce eyes and full breasts. Something of her jewelry caught the light of a cooking fire before she vanished. She must have been with child before Nsumbu was taken to Kinshasa. He could not have known. I realize now that if there was a sorrow in me, as I held Nsumbu's child against my breast, it was because I felt that I had missed my chance. Where Johnny Malebo had quietly torn himself apart, my child with Her would have been resplendent as the birth of a black messiah, and all our days would have been glad. The forces that would threaten any other man with confusion and despair would be silent in him, my progeny. He would have been the foundation of a happier race. Instead, Nsumbu doted on the boy, so simple and damned.

Her soiled womb—my spent pride—a consummation devoutly to be wished—I went out into the prodigious jungle. There are villages along the spidery inlets and gothic interstitial arteries. When the Company established this station, during the ivory culls and deforestation, the government of my predecessor and the mercenary insurgency of my Rival, the villages had been abandoned. Those that had not been deserted were stripped and exploited, leaving malformed cavities along the banks like gold teeth ripped crudely from gums. In the months after my Ascension, the hovels were tentatively reclaimed, and inhabited again. In those ambiguous pavilions of reeds and clay, a new species has emerged: men and women without hands, amputees with truncated limbs like sealed wax, these deformations reminiscent of the return of a forgotten malaise—monstrous children waving blunt limbs from the vivid mangroves. There is a sorrow as contagious as disease. Though their bodies suggest their pygmy antecedents, and the structure of their skulls recalls certain agonies of prehistory, their wrist stumps are now, irrevocably—*Belgian*—

The marshes were scattered with tobacco-shaded corpses. There, also, one found this species of dark man, weird Hominini whose necks seemed to have grown metal collars, heavy yokes of rusted iron. These collars coupled endangered families together as efficiently as railway carriages. Because I am *nzambi,* I tampered with their evolutionary selection, removing these exterior links whenever I could, setting this bedeviled nocturnal race back thousands of years in the colonial mind—an aboriginal abjection of the white lines of progress, leaving upon these Africans only the spectral manacles of natural ignorance.

*Limbs as black as iron—sucking gun barrels—sailing my paper boat—*I lived in the villages with them for a long time. It was established on the shore where part of the river opened into a lake that the natives called Luango. They picked over my body for lice and were much amused by the prospect of their pallid god sharing their shambolic huts. I killed for them with my Remington. A gang of them butchered a white rhinoceros on the spot where I blasted it, before dragging gargantuan slabs of carcass through the brackens and ferns to their fire pit. It had been drinking at a shallow pond of rainwater when I encountered it. Awestruck at its Pliocene armor and the crescent of horn reflected on the silver water, I contemplated the arbitrary cruelty of shooting it. The weapon in my hands, braced against a tree split by old lightning, was from an industrial era that the abused Negroes might never know for themselves. But elsewhere the imperial factories and the bodies of man were conniving, coinciding, evolving as one toward a distant obsolescence. Homo sapiens were moving toward that horrific rim I had seen in my sickness, extinction. Reluctantly, I pulled the trigger and the slug thumped into the animal's gray head. For a moment, it stood still, engaged in a pitiful effort to turn its massive face toward me, questioning, confused. Then, it splashed against the edge of the pond, hemorrhaging from a ragged hole close to its opposite ear. I recall the way the villagers cried out and streamed from the shadows behind me, those that still possessed one or two hands. The meat was hard and almost inedible to me, but these queer villagers ruminated upon it for minutes at a time, straining some tenderness from the scorched flesh.

At night, there was primordial music, and some of the people danced around the fire. They smoked pipes of green hemp and brought me clay vessels of palm beer. I knew that my heart could never weary of such places. I lay upon my back in the dirt of the delta, staring at the pinprick stars, and the parallax of bright embers before them, the Milky Way and the ghostly fumes of fading lives rising toward it. I listened to the women and children singing, and the profound sweetness and perfect anomie of that repose compassed all my wicked white pores, as though love had staked me to the earth—

When at last I returned to the station, I found it in disarray. Extinguished fires smoldered between the huts, the crack of the last boiling sap the only sound. A section of the tree line had been destroyed, as if Company dynamite had been planted there, shredding the trunks down to their cores of amber heartwood. Leafless branches had been sheared and blown across the sloping ground. Obscuring my view down to the river, a silver plume hung over the scene before me. As I moved through the coal-mist, I saw that certain of the huts had been razed, and shrapnel of clay and struts was strewn across the lawn. I glanced toward my station house and found it intact and undamaged. My first fear, that some of my Rival's men were still roaming and had returned for revenge, faded at that discovery. Surely, they would have burned my barracks to the ground. Could it be the Company? The eerie silence persisted, even as I came closer to the water, where a group of more than a dozen Negroes surrounded some large object, with their kinky heads bowed. "Nsumbu, Junker, *wapi sika*? Where are they?" Not one of the men turned toward the sound of my voice. They were hypnotized. When I was directly behind them, I heard a gentle weeping from some of them. Finally, as I stepped through the stiff mob, I beheld the object of their attention. It was an adolescent bull elephant, and it was solidly, absolutely dead. Its jowl was stained with the viscous effluvium of musth, tacky as molasses—a sluggish drip from the gray space behind its eye. It sparkled like misplaced tears that death had not stopped, finding its way along the rivulets of flesh to the gaping triangular mouth. The trunk lay as if probing toward the water. The tusks were coated in dirt, and the enormous bulk of the animal reeked of its own excrement. Spoor had spattered the grass where it fell. I walked around it, on the waterside, and saw the fist-sized bullet hole and the swollen exploded lobes of the brain. Under the left tusk were several smaller bore wounds that could not have prevented the creature's rage. Flies shimmered in the awful jam. I slapped the tusks with my palm, telling the men: "Get my ivory!" Initially, none of them stirred. One of the ones who had been weeping raised his arm painfully, pointing toward my station house.

When I opened the door, I found Nsumbu and Junker inside. Nsumbu's wife was with them. The scene imposed itself upon me immediately, with a violent pang of agony. The wild elephant had trampled the infant. Nsumbu cradled his dead child, a pulverized membrane of black, with all the bones in splinters. They had wiped away the viscera from the rent where the ribs had been. The boy was nothing now, but an appalling effigy. I wanted every elephant dead. The grief in the room was a relentless pulse. It came from the chthonic clays beneath the station and rose into us as poisonous sap, rooting us to the inescapable Congo, the genocide of our dreams. And, worst of all, they all looked at me, imploring my divinity, as if something could be done—

"Exterminate all the brutes!"

The prodigal massacre of the elephants would continue until the station collapsed under the weight of ivory. I shot them down with vengeance, as if the sanctity of universe depended upon it. We gave the hollow child what rites we could. His tiny skull remains in my garden. As the bloodshed continued, certain of the chiefs of the charcoal tribes that had been subdued and dormant began to come to my station. They were squeamish, you understand? With Nsumbu in his decaying uniform as my interlocutor, I listened dully to their entreaties. It cost Nsumbu to listen to these crawling witchdoctors and their gaudy monarchs. He shook as I sent my refusals through him, but was fortified by the disappointment in their eyes. I dismissed them tersely, and sent them back to their tribal holes, where they could listen to my gunfire and the extinction of the elephants like frightened children listening to their father beating their mother beyond flimsy floral wallpaper. One delegation of six I cut down with my revolver, for they upset him excessively. Could the bastards not see that we had lost our son? The singular tribe that resisted this squeamishness was that of my votaries from the lake. The Russian withdrew, but returned, and withdrew again. His oscillations between the station and his downriver hovel increased. I neglected the station.

The hanged man—forgotten riverine tribes—It was not quite dawn when Nsumbu woke me this morning. He had cast off the blue Company uniform and its rotting allusions to gold. He had not removed it in my presence since I adopted him in Kinshasa. He lit a match and ignited the dregs of a kerosene lamp. I saw the elongated shadow of a pair of horns roll across the ceiling where the dew now dripped in.

"Mistah Kurtz, *lufwa*?"

I caught the word for the decline into death. "Not yet, Nsumbu."

The savage smiled. He was naked. The man had painted his entire body with vivid scarlet clay. The magnificence that had impressed itself upon me so profoundly when I watched him kill Vicious Boy, illuminated with witch-flames, was returned to him, even as he stood over me with shimmering tears dripping mercury from his bones. He wore an antelope scalp and the crooked horns glowed in the kerosene. I lay in my soddened bed, the slow ache in my knee, mesmerized as he waved a mangled totem over my fever, still holding the lamp in his other hand. The control he exerted over his own conflict was such that no emotion could burst from me when I comprehended the bizarre object hovering in my sight. What he passed over me was a chimera of raven feathers, splayed sticks like a small kite, and the grotesque skin of his trampled child. Under his low incantations, this shocking black flag I apprehended with a kind of relief, or fathomless gratitude. I did not move, but kept my eyes fixed on the tenebrous bat's wing that the boy's empty flesh had become.

She entered after him, her naked form filigreed in rings of glimmering brass wire. Her hair had been cut into a fierce frame about her tawny features. Brass is a Company currency, and now, it was as if she possessed all of it, a Cleopatra with her snake-wrapped forearm, reaching in anguish for her melanistic breast. I saw that her brow was smeared with rouge paint, and she was otherwise draped in an eclectic shawl of fetishes and amulets. In the amber gloom of my station, they watched over me, so degenerate, so regnant. Nsumbu passed the child-skin monstrosity over my face again and extinguished the lamp. A single shaft of sunlight bored through a crack in the ceiling.

Presently, the Russian opened the screen door and invited himself in. When he saw the royals over my bed, he was aghast. Something fell from his grasp and smashed at his feet. Raising myself upon my elbows, I observed him staring forlornly at the broken glass and the liquid stain spreading across the warped floorboards. He was trembling. Thin sounds of panic escaped him. "That was the last of it," he whimpered. "These two can't help you with the pain." They turned upon him. She cursed him for interrupting their witchcraft and struck him with her fists. I labored out of my bed as the Russian fled the decaying station house, and I watched as he collapsed outside on the grass, barely a few feet beyond my garden, curled into a febrile, fetal knot. I almost laughed. Neither medicinal science, nor the abject sorcery of the jungle, had been permitted to do their work. There was nothing remaining for me, save for my ideas. Nsumbu and his wife governed the abyss when I was away, and I let them both live in the remains of the Company quarters. Finally, they must have evicted the capricious Russian.

Sunrise, indigo to pink—I was standing erect within the eviscerated corpse of an elephant, the titanic gray sheath of its hide flowing out behind me, as I forced my head upward, through the smashed plates of the cranium, into the bloody hollow where the brain had been. All of the other bones had been stripped. The beast I wore splayed out in one giant cadaverous robe, as I became its spine, skull and operator. It was mine to work like an oriental under his paper dragon. Then, slowly, from some instinct, I pushed my hands, my forearms and then the full extent of my arms down into the tusks, until I was clad to my shoulders. As I strove to enter them, their weird marrow slopped out like blue clay.

Strange mechanical sounds filtered in through the massive ears, a wet reverberation. I wanted to look out, but the eyes were set too far apart and the jellies were too dark and thick. Instead, I stared out from the hole in the brow, blown by my exploding bullet, engulfed in gore, the shifting of flies, and the awful fumes of putrescence. I tried to raise the tusks, so that I might advance toward the river. The water emitted its odd music. The effort of raising my arms in the hard shafts threatened to overwhelm me. I saw my own back ripping open under the great weight and my vertebrae spilling like white coins from the rented skin. At first, and for a long time, I was the only human tenant of my dream as I staggered forth in the too heavy flesh. I moved closer to the water. I said to myself, I suppose that it is the elephants, not the hyenas, becoming my conscience, impossible to bear. Through the large bullet hole, the sunlight was fierce. The day elapsed in sudden flashes, until, at dusk, I glimpsed the Station. It was burning. Flames and brilliant cinders rose into the darkening sky. The terrible epidermis dragged behind me, a leaden sheet painting a red stain across the earth. I thought, perhaps I could fill the trunk with water and put out the fire. Then, as I watched from the ragged makeshift eye, I saw that a boat was approaching along the channel. It was the mechanical sound that I had heard at the beginning. A steamer was coming slowly through the choked tributary to my Station. There was a white man standing in the bow. I saw him with the euphoria of a dying man who feels his pain suddenly eclipsed. The smoke from the fire must have cleared slightly, for he suddenly observed me. From within my vile costume, I tried to cry out to him, but suffocation prevented me. I realized further that I could recall none of the languages that I had ever spoken. I swung my collapsed head toward him, the impotent trunk trawling back between my legs as some satanic tail. I held my arms aloft, triumphantly encased in their white armor. A thin black figure stood beside him on the deck, raising a Winchester. I remember a spear arcing through the smoke. The white man on the steamer opened his mouth to scream—

There are rumors, Chinese whispers along the sycophantic chains of the Company, that I am to be arraigned. Kurtz is to be rescinded—my ideas have become paralogical. It is difficult to regard these accounts seriously, since one simple whisper is milled into so many split grains of half-truth, yet perhaps there is one grain of truth amongst them. The Company is disturbed: good! I have got above my station. Montagu is reluctant to bite the hand that feeds, but he is beginning to starve. Janssens stares at inexplicable blank spaces in his account ledgers. Rommel tells the restive pilgrims that my errant cannibalism and uncivilized resistance are delaying the completion of the railway behind the rapids. Émile is recovering mysterious and salacious correspondence from the *Telegraph* concerning the Hannibal of Jamaica Road, and even tokens from you, My Intended, with your childlike fidelity to our future. I can only imagine that Johnny Malebo is blotting my copybook with some erratic memoir, or scandalous pamphlet—*Let it come down*—I am writing this in the rain, on the shore of Lake Luango, beneath the rattling leaves of a lean-to. My people are melancholy. To the extent that time persists here, we are running low. The Company will come after me. It is inevitable. I don't want them here. Therefore, while these rumors continue, I must return to the station. I have more than one disease uncoiling in me, and the Company will want me alive, so there is that. Eric Paine got out, and returned. When this rain passes, I will instruct my people in the construction of a litter to bear me back to the skull garden, the decaying veranda, and the river. Meanwhile, I must shave my head and prepare my sickening body.

They carried me between creaking poles, where I rose and fell like an ecstatic breath—my Jubilee procession, thin and prodigal Kurtz borne like the husk of Leopold along the muddy avenues of his country. The forest murmured as I went, and the bright birds hung on a desolate breeze. There was a burst of distant gunfire. The crackling report of it was certainly low-caliber, anxious travellers, not hunters. But I thought of the dying bull elephant with the sunken back and the broken teeth. We were the same in nature, shadowed by our younger kin toward Acheron. Even before we broke the green fringe to the station, I perceived the familiar drone and slap of a Company steamer. The coincidence made me anxious. I had wanted to reach the station before them and to receive them in my barrack, where I could stand up, leaning against the mantel if necessary, or with a cane to support myself. The cost of carrying my disease was our late arrival. I ordered my bearers to set me down, yet they resisted. In that terminal moment, as I raged, their hearts were broken. I implored them to abandon me, to leave me to the Company and to go back to the tranquility of their lake. But they fanned out of the long grass in a terminal gesture of warlike defiance. Helpless, I thought of Richardson and had a vision of him dressed in his white ship steward's uniform, turning the ratchet on his Gatling gun at the Zulus—*you'll know what the Devil feels like in his finest moments of cruelty—fifty skulls exploding right in front of you, blood and brains washing over the veldt*—My eyes were washed with tears as they lowered my litter to the earth. Settling my cheek against my shoulder, down the slope within a knot of pilgrims and slaves, I recognized Nikolai Junker standing on the deck of the steamer with Montagu, and the man I had seen arriving in my dreams.

Better at the Lake—dressed in calico, dispensing eternity and gin—Ma Albert was in the hospital. She suffered a stroke. This I learned from one of the correspondences Montagu had intercepted and retained at his station in Léopoldville. There was even a letter from Maybrick, who has apparently returned to hanging around the Thames like a guilty thing. Montagu has me confined in a cabin on their steamer. A serpent of laudanum is still investigating my arteries. During the afternoon, while the manager supervised the confiscation of my ivory, I was attended to by this man Marlow. He was wearing the Company uniform, but with a pair of velvet slippers. He had a stricken, boyish aspect, as though his flesh had suddenly outrun his mind, or vice versa, the stigmata of abrupt and brutal experience having disordered his conscience. A jaundiced pallor had settled in him, and was, even as we smoked his tobacco in the cabin, drawing the youth from his cheeks, contracting his brow. The weight of his fascination was palpable, as was the ache of his present inability to voice it. Part of Marlow had receded. I explained everything to him, which is to say that I could not give him anything: "We live as we dream—alone . . ." *Yet, I had dreamed of Marlow.* Eventually, he pushed one of the letters to me across the sheets. It was on Company stationary, with a Belgian stamp overlapped by a dozen red postmarks. Evidently, he had anticipated its contents. The Brussels office recommended Marlow, in ways that his physical presence did not, as the agent to bring me in. I told him that I was pleased for him. In fact, I was. I conceived of the possibility of my life in him. He reminded me of Édouard Kurtz in Calais, embracing a corpse and dragging it to the water. "I'm glad," I said.

The curtain was pulled back and Montagu, that fatuous collection of mediocrities, stepped inside the cabin. Marlow rose briskly, guiltily, and left as though the two of them were counterparts of a clockwork mechanism. After drawing the curtain behind him, Montagu seated himself awkwardly upon a campstool. He wiped his face with a handkerchief. "What are they doing, Kurtz? Your niggers are all along the embankment. Did you summon them to prevent us from taking you?"

"I have no influence over them. They're cannibals, you know?"

Montagu fumed. "Listen, you bastard," he said, "I'm trying to save what remains of your white skin. The Russian informs me that—"

I remained laconic. "Don't listen to Junker, man. The mongrel was nearly drowned, almost executed. His brain is damaged. He is in shock, perpetual shock. He lies compulsively."

"I demand to know what they're doing out there."

"You're a bloody coward, Montagu. You're not at all interested in their reasons. The only reason that you are in here interrogating me is because you are afraid to be out on the deck."

"But, I'm trying to save you, Kurtz."

Then I wished that Nsumbu would attack the steamer, but I knew that he would not. What else did the poor devil desire, but to live out his days? A mourning beat over the encroaching darkness of the station, encompassing everything in a profound stillness. I had my yellow book of poems.

Je meurs de lassitude. C'est le tombeau, je m'en vais aux vers, horreur de l'horreur! Satan, farceur, tu veux me dissoudre, avec tes charmes. Je réclame. Je réclame! Un coup de fourche, une goutte de feu.

Outside, latent crocodiles encircle the boat where I am a prisoner. Steamer and station complain under the burden of ivory, yet the best of it remains in my pleasure dome. A slow drumming reverberates through the raffia palms, the torpid trance-inducing pulse of an expiring giant attended by pygmies. It is almost midnight. This Marlow fancies himself as Saint Christopher, and he'll serve any devil until he discovers what the new devil is afraid of, waiting on whatever intimidates him with a tenuous, dislocative loyalty. Now, he has come to believe that he can carry me out of the torrent of my dying. And if I die, what will he do? I cannot pity him. When I vanish, he will understand that there are many devils and many servants. The crone moves toward the blinds—Close the shutter. I can't bear to look at this. I have progressed into the time of the assassins.

Sleep has overcome the white men like the gesture of a plague.
  It is time for me to get out, and to crawl toward my Pit.
  How does one forget the future, once witnessed?
  My ivory throne stands in the magpie night.
  I am alone in the heartbeat of the Congo.
  Korzeniowski. Are you all right?
  This must be my final report.
  I govern the abyss.
  Korzeniowksi?
  —Kurtz.

MISTAH KURTZ!

JAMES REICH is the author of two previous novels, *Bombshell* (2013) and *I, Judas* (2011), both published by Soft Skull Press. He is Chair of Creative Writing and Literature at Santa Fe University of Art and Design, and a member of PEN American Center and the International Association of Crime Writers: North America. Reich's work has been published by *The Rumpus, Salon.com, The Nervous Breakdown, Sensitive Skin, International Times, The Weeklings, Fiction Advocate,* and others. He is also the editor-in-chief of Stalking Horse Press as well as a founding member of the band Venus Bogardus with vinyl and CD releases on independent record labels in the US and UK. Born in England in 1971, Reich has been a resident of the US since 2009. He is represented by Lippincott, Massie, McQuilkin literary agents. Visit him online at **www.jamesreichbooks.com**.

CPSIA information can be obtained
at www.ICGtesting.com
Printed in the USA
LVOW11s0143170417
530968LV00001B/17/P